Plowed

Blue Collar Bad Boys, Volume 7

Brill Harper

Published by Brill Harper, 2017.

PLOWED

First edition. December 1, 2017.

Copyright © 2017 Brill Harper.

ISBN: 979-8223149033

Written by Brill Harper.

About this Book

After serving five years of a ten-year sentence for a crime I didn't commit, coming home after being vindicated should be my triumph. All I want is the life I was supposed to have as the once golden boy of this town—a thriving farm, a strong family, and a house full of kids. I guess I should have learned by now that nothing is fair, and I'll have to work just as hard to make it on the outside as I did to survive in prison.

The fields are fallow, my house is falling down around my nearly catatonic father, and my ex-girlfriend is somebody else's wife now. But I'm not giving up. I'll replant the crops, fix the house, and find a wife. Not in that order, because a man has needs, and mine have been denied too long.

The quirky, extra-curvy waitress at the diner could use someone looking out for her, and I need a favor in return. Starting with a baby.

This farmer is about to take a wife.

I hope she's ready for me.

Author's Confession: Well, there's a lot of plowing and seeding on the farm, yeah? Prepare yourself accordingly.

(If you like alpha hero, bbw heroine, insta-everything set in a small town you are set.)

Chapter One

Boone

It's not like I expected a homecoming parade when I rolled back into this dusty little town of Hazel in Eastern Washington. It would have been nice to have gotten a ride home from the fucking bus station though.

I don't know why Pops wasn't there at the station to pick me up as planned. He hasn't sounded like himself on our weekly phone calls, and he stopped visiting me years ago when Mom took sick.

I hitched a ride as far as the mailbox on the main road, but it's another mile up the driveway to the house. Which gives me time to think. Too much time.

What might have been. If I'd never been falsely imprisoned. If my mom had lived to see me vindicated—the real criminal finally arrested. Damn. The familiar anger churns through my gut knowing my mom died without me at her bedside. At least I know her faith in me never wavered. Not once. She always believed I was innocent and never stopped praying for justice to be served. I only wish it could have happened when she was alive to see it. What I wouldn't give for one more day. One last chance to hold her hand. To tell her they found the real criminal and let me out.

The fields along the driveway are sick. I don't need to use my bachelor's degree in ag science to know that. Why hadn't Pops gotten more help with them? As I round the last corner, my childhood home looms in the distance. It seems sad. Forgotten. Jesus. I've only been gone for five years—I didn't think a house could change so much. Though five years on the inside seemed a lot longer to me, too.

There are no flowers anywhere the eye can see. Mom used to keep up the beds circling the house so there was always color no matter what the season. I wonder what happened to the furniture that used to be on the front porch. That was the place I was always guaranteed to find my folks in the evening after supper, at least until the weather got too cold for even cocoa and lap blankets to keep them warm on their porch swing. Now the screen door is propped up against the wall to the right of the door, and all the windows are closed despite the pleasant spring breeze. No curtains are open to let in the light, either.

I open the door and it creaks like a damned haunted house. I take a few steps in. It's musty when it used to smell like lemon furniture wax with hints of cinnamon from the kitchen. There are newspapers and magazines stacked haphazardly down the sticky hallway floor that used to shine like a mirror.

"Pops?" I yell out. "You home?"

I stop at the wall of portraits. I hardly know the young kid smiling so big with his first fish, his first blue ribbon, his first prom date. There he is with his football championship trophy. Another with his high school diploma. Look at him standing between his parents in his university graduation gown. He's got the whole world in front of him.

Six months later, all that promise would be gone. Taken from him. Wrenched out of his life.

The last time someone took my picture, it was when they were booking me on bogus charges. I haven't been a free man since. I'm not sure I feel free now.

"Pops?" I find him in his recliner. Stacks of newspapers and empty beer cans circle the chair. He's snoozing while the baseball game plays on the television with no sound. I gently shake his shoulder. "Pops?"

He snorts as he wakes up, trying to place where he is and who is talking to him. "Boone? Is that you?"

"Of course, it's me."

His eyes don't seem to focus. "I thought I was picking you up tomorrow?"

He smells like he's been bathing in old beer.

"That was today, Pops."

His skin is too yellow and his eyes too red. He looks doughy and slow, so unlike the man I remember. Five years. How could everything change so much in five years? He grunts. "Sorry, son. I guess I lost track of the days. I was going to clean up this mess today...before you got here..." He trails off as we both take in the mess and realize it would have taken him far more than one day to clean up.

My guess is he's been living in this chair since he buried Mom three years ago.

"What do I care about a little mess? It's good to see you," I lie. I love him more than I can say, but it's not good to see him. Not like this. This man is broken.

Just one more thing taken from me. My childhood hero.

"You look..."

I chuckle. "Big. Yeah, I had a lot of time to exercise." I'd been in good shape for my entire life, the way an athlete is, but in prison, I had to get stronger. Bigger. Meaner. I'm one scary son of a bitch now. The golden boy this town remembers died the day he was arrested. This man I am now is the kind of guy you find in a roadhouse biker bar, not the quarterback on the field or the prom king on the dance floor.

"You hungry, Pops? I could sure use some grub."

He shakes his head. "I'll just have another beer."

"Sure thing. I'll bring it to you."

My mom's kitchen is destroyed. Garbage everywhere—mostly food wrappers and beer cans. A lot of flies are circling the sink full of dirty dishes. Rage fills my chest instead of air. Not at my dad—he's obviously sick. I knew he was depressed when we spoke on the phone, but to be confronted with what it looks like in real life, to see how lost he's been without his wife. Without his son.

No, the rage is at the unfairness. The life I was supposed to have compared to this one. This dirty, neglected place that used to shine. The house without its heart. I know my mom still might have gotten cancer and died if I'd been here—but Pops and I would have had each other to get us through it. Instead, he got sicker and I got meaner.

I bring him his beer and make a meal out a couple cheap frozen dinners cooked in a microwave so heavy with grime I wonder why it hasn't caught fire. Later, I get my dad in his own bed instead of the recliner I'm afraid he sleeps on every night. I don't sleep in my old room. I can't even go in there yet. I can't face the old Boone right now. He's a ghost. I sleep in one of the guest rooms instead. And I start making plans.

I have a lot of living to catch up on. A lot of work to go along with it. Work is good. It will keep me from thinking about what I used to have. What I should have now by all rights.

Thanks to the internet, I know my ex-girlfriend is married with one kid and one on the way. Her husband is a high school friend. Or was. Neither he nor Amy ever visited me in prison. They have a farm, and I have fallow fields. They have kids, and I have an aging hero in a recliner who looks ready to be put out to pasture. They look happy. In love.

I have my hand for companionship.

As I rub one out, for necessity not pleasure, it sure feels like I've traded one damn prison for another.

Madeline

I'M GOOD AT A LOT OF things. Okay, not really a lot. But waiting tables isn't one of them. Lord knows I try, though. I hate being on the receiving end of Big Mac's tirades.

I'm pouring fresh water for table four when I hear Mac from the kitchen. "Madeliiiinne!"

I flinch. And knock over the water glass. Which of course lands in the lap of my customer. Who jumps up and starts yelling at me. Which causes their baby to start crying. I should be grabbing a towel or apologizing or running to the exit never to return. Instead, I stand there. With my mouth open at the havoc I'm causing.

I am the worst waitress in the world. It's not news to anyone that eats here. And Big Mac is pretty aware of my shortcomings, too. He only keeps me here because his wife won't let him fire me. Not that Vera cares about me all that much, either. It's just that she has misplaced loyalty to me. Or maybe it's guilt.

Strangely, as I'm trying to apologize to the people at table four, everything in the diner gets quiet.

Like those old westerns on TV when the gunslinger enters the saloon and all heads turn and the music stops, everyone in Big Mac's Diner pauses in mid-action like we've been practicing the mannequin challenge for a week. The radio is still kicking out a classic rock song from the '80s, and something sizzles loudly on the grill, but those are the only sounds. Even the baby snuffled up her last wail.

We're all looking at the door—just a regular glass door, not the swinging shutters from an old-time saloon. Standing there, blocking the sun, is the Hulk, I think. Well, he's not green. He's just huge. Muscles bulge out from places mere mortals don't have muscles.

I'm equal parts in awe of him and in fear of him. In fact, I'm mapping my way to the kitchen exit and looking for cover in case there's violence. His expression doesn't exactly say he's here for a cheeseburger and a Coke.

Oh my God.

I recognize him. That's Boone Barker. Word is that he was released from prison last week, but sightings have been scarce. Not that anyone could blame him for staying away since nobody got out the welcome wagon for the poor guy. The opposite, in fact. It would have made everyone feel a whole lot better if he'd just never come back. Then they wouldn't have to face how badly they treated him. How everyone just forgot about him and left him to rot in that cell only to find out he's not guilty after all.

Which is pretty shitty, when you think about it.

He doesn't make eye contact with anyone as he starts walking the rest of the way inside. When he takes a seat at a booth, I realize maybe he really is here for a cheeseburger and a Coke.

Shit! He's in my section.

I shoot a pleading glance at Marion to cover me, but she shakes her head. Most days, I expect her to say things like, "Kiss my grits," with that nicotine voice she's got. But despite the hard lines on her face, she's usually pretty nice to me.

I mouth the word "please" but Marion shakes her head.

Damn.

I already suck at this job when I'm not half scared to death. I can't imagine how many ways I'll find to screw this up.

Boone Barker is seven years older than my twenty. I remember following his championship football season when I was in middle school and he was a senior. Every girl with a beating heart had a crush on Boone Barker. He was the quarterback, the prom king, the valedictorian—basically he was the kind of guy that nobody believes exists in real life. Perfect. Handsome. Smart. Friendly. Talented.

They took his picture out of the trophy case at the high school when he was arrested.

I just assumed he was guilty. Otherwise, it would have been unbearable to think about—our hometown hero in prison for no reason. It was easier to believe he'd gone rogue than to accept that life could be that unfair.

Turns out life really is that horrible.

He was innocent the whole time.

His sentence has been overturned, and he's a free man now. He should look a lot happier than he does. If I were him, I'd have settled someplace new. Where they didn't used to know and supposedly love me and then turn their backs on me. Where they wouldn't turn their eyes away in guilt at their own shame whenever I come near.

But I don't have a family of my own anymore, and Boone does, which is probably what brought him back. He's got his dad and that farm. Both are a mess from what I hear, but at least it's something. Me? I've got a crappy room above Big Mac's garage out back, a job I'm no good at that makes less than nothing, and a family of me, myself, and I.

I swallow hard against the ball of fear in my throat. Everyone around me gets back to their business, though their tones are hushed. Marion brings out a towel for my soaked customer, and I shuffle slowly to Boone's table.

I pull the pad out of my pocket and the pen from behind my ear. "Welcome to Big Mac's," I say, too loudly I bet because my ears are ringing, and I'm probably going to throw up on him or faint dead away on the floor, "What can I get for you?"

He studies me for what seems like a really long time. He's still handsome, but it's grittier now. My heartbeat fills my ears, which is better than the ringing, I guess. His stare is so intense, though. Like I can physically feel the testosterone emitting out of his gaze.

I break eye contact, but there's no safe place for my gaze to roam. His square, stubbled jaw. The thick column of his throat. His broad shoulders stretch the very limits of his T-shirt seams. His barrel chest. His...

He coughs, and I blink back my perusal. Is he smiling at me? Just a little? You can't really tell by his mouth, but his eyes soften just a bit. "A menu."

"Huh?" I sputter.

"You asked what you could get me. I'd like to start with a menu."

"Of course." Stupid, Madeline. "Sorry. I'll..." I point to the counter. "And then...right back I'll be."

Right back I'll be?

I repeat my stupidness all the way to the counter, where I manage to remember to grab a menu and the coffee pot in case he wants some, and back to his table. *Right back I'll be.* I really am hopeless.

I hand him a menu and ask if he wants coffee. He eyes my shaking hand and says no. I leave him to take care of my remaining tables and try to compose myself.

Why am I so flustered? He's the one who is trying to get his life back after a horrible mistake. Everyone should be trying to make him feel at home instead of ostracizing him because they feel bad they weren't on his side when he needed them most.

"Have you decided?" I ask when I work up the nerve to go back to his table.

"Cheeseburger and a Coke." He did not just say that. Did he really? "You have a nice smile," he adds.

I hadn't realized I was smiling. "Thanks. You have nice hands."

Oh. My. God. Seriously, I need a muzzle. I'd just been looking at his hands, and so it came out. I can't even fathom what I'd meant to say.

"Thanks."

Count it off, Maddy Mae. Three. Two. One.

I take a breath after my silent counting and try again. "I'm sorry. I'd love to say that I'm not usually so awkward, but this is pretty much how I just am. So, I'll just go and put your order in."

"And right back you'll be?"

I can't help but laugh. "Something like that, yeah."

When I bring his Coke, he's staring out the window. It doesn't seem fair that he looks so sad when he should be happy to be out of prison. "Has very much changed? It always looks all the same to me. Day in, day out."

He blinks at me. Wow. I don't know that I ever realized how deep a green his eyes were. Probably not since this is the closest I've ever been to him.

"It's kind of weird. It's the same but different. That probably doesn't make any sense." He slides his drink closer. "Thanks for asking. Not many people have acknowledged that I've been gone or that I'm back."

"You deserve better than that. I'm sorry, Boone. I'm so sorry that you had to go to prison and that it took so long to find the evidence to prove your innocence. I'm sorry for all you've lost. And I'm really sorry that people don't know how to treat you now. It's not your fault."

"Well, it's not their fault either. I'm not the same man they knew." Something about the way he looks at me makes my heart do a little flip. "On the bright side, I do have nice hands, though."

My cheeks flame out. "You like teasing me."

"It's been a long time since I've been able to tease a pretty girl."

"Now I know you're teasing." Pretty girl. Ha. "I'm not beating off the boys from my front door." Oh. My. God. "I said that out loud, didn't I?" He nods. "I'll go check on your burger and maybe sew my mouth closed so I stop saying stupid things."

He laughs through his nose. "I like the way you talk. You say what you're thinking. It's not a quality a lot of people have these days. A person knows where he stands with someone who doesn't hide what they're thinking in words they don't mean."

"Well, what I'm thinking right now is your lunch must be close to ready. I'll go see if I can add some extra fries to your plate without anyone noticing."

He winks at me, and I concentrate on my steps so I don't humiliate myself further by tripping.

Marion stops me behind the counter. "Is he going to start trouble?"

"What? No. He's minding his own business. Which is more than I can say for all the gawkers in here. Hasn't the poor man been through enough?"

Marion shakes her head; her stiff updo never moves, though. I wonder how much of her paycheck goes to hairspray. Whatever is left from her Menthol Mores. "Look at him, though. He looks like those guys from *Sons of Anarchy*."

"He does not." Except in the very best way possible. "He looks like he's lifted a lot of weights and is ready to take care of his farm."

The bell rings and Mac shouts, "Order up!" I grab the burger and make my way to Boone, but not before I hear Mac bellow my name again. Great. What did I do now?

I'll...just ignore him for a bit.

"Madeline, how come I don't recognize you?" Boone asks me, reading my name tag when I set his plate down and pull the ketchup from my pocket.

"It's Madeline, with a long *I*, actually. And we didn't go to school at the same time." Not that he would have recognized me if we had. I had an awkward stage more awkward than the one I'm in now. And it lasted a good long while.

"Wait," he grabs my wrist, his eyes lighting up with curiosity, "are you *Mad Maddy*?"

Fuck. Me. I hate this town.

Tugging my arm away from him, I knock the ketchup bottle over. "Will that be everything?" I ask through clenched teeth. Fuck. Fuck. Fuck

Boone rights the bottle. "I'm sorry. That was rude of me." I shrug and turn, but he grabs my wrist again. "Madeline, I'm sorry."

"It really doesn't matter."

"No, it does. It's just that there aren't many people in this town more notorious than me. I didn't mean to be rude, though."

There's nothing I can do about the hot ball of tears working its way up. "Nobody has called me that to my face in a long time."

It was my dad who was notorious. Every town has one. I just drew the lucky lottery ticket and got to be the daughter of the crazy guy who would stand on the street corner and rail at all the sins of man, prophesizing doomsday. My mom left me with him when I was too small to remember her. I don't begrudge her escaping him. I just wish she'd taken me with her.

Every weekend, I had to stand on the corner with him, holding up my sign. I didn't know what they even meant for a long time. I didn't know we were abnormal. That all fathers weren't so stern, so full of hate. He was probably mentally ill, too, but it's hard to work up compassion for the man who kept me prisoner to his strict religion.

We'd lived on the outskirts of town, off grid. He did odd jobs and I did the housework once I was old enough. When I questioned his anger at people we didn't even know, I had to write pages and pages of bible verses. So I stopped asking questions. As I got older, I realized people called us Lunatic Larry and Mad Maddy.

I had to wear long dresses that looked like I was a frontier girl and was home-schooled until junior high when the state forced him to put me into the system he so hated. Going to public school, as you might imagine, was not a picnic. Kids are cruel. And so was my dad. But little by little, I was able to loosen myself from his tight grip. I made a friend. Then two. They would help me change in the bathroom before school started, into clothes they brought me from home. A teacher took pity on me and would sneak me books that I could escape into as long as I kept them hidden from my father.

"Will you forgive me for being such a douchebag?" Boone asks.

"It's no big deal."

"No, it really is. I got mean in prison. I don't want to stay that way. Please tell me what I can do to earn your forgiveness."

"Madeliiiiine!"

We both look toward the kitchen. "I have to go. Enjoy your meal."

With any luck, I'll never see Boone Barker again. Of course, the only luck I've ever had is bad.

Chapter Two

Boone

I've been home two months now, and every day feels like I'm getting further behind than ahead.

I can't do it all. The house, the fields, my dad. They all need one hundred percent of my attention, but I don't have three hundred percent to give.

Staring at the yellow legal pad in front of me isn't helping move things along, but the words just aren't coming together the way I want them to. I keep getting distracted by my too-young waitress with the cool gray eyes and round, curvy body.

My cock is not happy that I've been out of prison for two months and haven't gotten it wet yet. I keep telling myself that's why I watch Madeline so close when I'm in the diner. Yeah, she's too young for me, but she's got the body of a woman. The kind I like. Soft and a little plump. She won't break under the weight of a big man. And she'd give him something to hold onto.

She's working through the tables, warming up coffee. Occasionally knocking things over or spilling things. It always makes me smile, though I'm smart enough not to let her see me doing it.

She's all wrong for me. But Jesus, those tits. I can hardly think about anything else sometimes.

"Whatcha working on there, Boone?" she asks when she gets to me.

The Big Mac's Diner T-shirt she's wearing is tight. She's got an apron on over it, but the view of side-boob I'm getting is making me hard. I really need to get laid. Soon. I wish I knew why I didn't go get some. I've seen the way women look at me. I could spend an evening in a bar and go home with one. I should. I could use a little softness in my life as much as my dick could use some pussy.

But that's not me. Not even the new me.

I was ready to marry my high school girlfriend before I was arrested. I never cheated, never wanted to. I don't want random sex—well, some of me does—and I'm not going to meet my future wife in a bar hook-up.

I flip the pad over so Madeline can't read it, so she shrugs and tops off my coffee. "Farm stuff," I explain.

"Top secret farm stuff?"

"Something like that."

I've come in to Big Mac's a few times a week, trying like hell to get used to people again. And to earn a smile or two from Madeline. They aren't easy to get. Not since I called her Mad Maddy that day. But I can't let it go. I need to get right with her, so I keep trying.

She was the first one in town to treat me normal, and I really screwed it up. I won't screw it up more by acting on my attraction to her. She deserves a chance at getting out of this town, not getting stuck here with someone even more notorious than her old man.

"Madeline, how's school going? You pass that test you were so worried about last week?"

There it is. That shy ghost of a smile. It's worth drinking the shitty coffee for. "I did."

"Never doubted you would. You're smart."

"Yeah, my brains have gotten me pretty far," she says, gesturing to the diner. "My maid is cleaning my mansion as we speak."

"Madeliiiine," Big Mac bellows from the kitchen.

"What is his problem with you?" I ask when she flinches at his voice. I don't like that. She's a good person. I feel like she's had a rough enough life without some asshole yelling at her all the time. "Big Mac needs to talk to you with more respect."

"I screw up a lot."

"Maybe you should try to get a different job. There are other restaurants in town."

She shakes her head. "I can't afford to go to school and pay rent somewhere. I work for room and board."

I clench my fist so hard that the pencil in my hand snaps. "They don't *pay* you?" Despite all that has happened to me, I have a strong sense of justice. Hell, maybe it's because of what happened to me.

Her eyes get big, and she picks up the half pencil that rolled onto the floor. "I get tips. Sometimes."

"That's not even legal." Big Mac is a hefty guy, but I can take him. I've taken bigger men out. Not something I guess I should be proud of, but if Madeline needs me for my muscle, I'm hers. "That's ridiculous that you don't earn a wage."

I'm so angry. If I could have one thing go my way, I'd use it to make sure she had a better life. She deserves more. I know we hardly know each other, but she brings out protective urges in me. Makes me feel like the kind of man I used to think I was.

"They're like family...sort of." She grimaces. "They were my last foster family just before I turned eighteen. They could have just tossed me out. But they let me rent a room above the garage in exchange for working here."

Shit. That's right. Her old man is dead. Though I can't say anyone probably mourned him. Maybe she does. I remember her dad. He was a vicious motherfucker, always condemning people to hell. It's hard to believe that little girl always at his side was my Madeline. I don't think she ever spoke to anybody back then. Just stood there mute and wearing a long pioneer dress next to her father. Her hair was always a nest of tangles, and her eyes too sunken for her face. It will always haunt me that I didn't try to help that little girl. Especially now that I know her. And like her. "How old were you when your dad died?"

"Fifteen." Oh, man. Alone so young.

"And you went into foster care."

"Look, this isn't really the conversation I want to have with my customer while I'm working."

"Maybe we're friends then."

She turns those gray eyes on me. There's no trust in them. "Right. Okay, friend. What are you hiding on that pad of paper then?"

"It's not important."

Her eyes go cold. "Sure thing. *Friend*."

"Madeline..."

"Boone, it's okay. But don't pretend we're buddies, okay? I'll respect your privacy and you respect mine. We just stick to things like the weather and if you want an English muffin or wheat toast."

Fuck. I should let it go. She's right, and the last thing I need is to get more obsessed with her anyway. I don't need to know more about her life. I don't need to get to know her better. What I should be concentrating on is getting my life back on track. And that means the house, the fields, and Pops. Not my curvy waitress.

Even as I am thinking all this, I flip the pad back over. "It's a Craigslist ad."

"You hiring on the farm?"

My dick is saying, "hell, yeah," at the thought of hiring Madeline. But no. She's too young. Isn't she?

"I'm looking for a wife."

Madeline

"YOU'RE HIRING A WIFE on Craigslist?" I know Big Mac is going to yell my name again any second, but I can't walk away now.

I set the coffee pot down and grab the pad before Boone can stop me.

Wife wanted: Woman in 20s needed to be farm wife. Needs to be able to cook basic meals and clean. Must want kids. Gardening a bonus.

"Oh, my God. You really are hiring a wife on Craigslist."

He scrubs his hand over his face. There are shadows under his eyes, but those eyes never stop moving. Like he's always expecting danger. Like he needs to defend himself all the time. "I need help. All the stuff my mom used to do...the cooking, cleaning, decorating...none of it gets done anymore. I can't do it all and work in the fields, too."

"Boone, you hire a cook or a maid or an interior decorator. You don't hire a wife."

"I have...needs...also. The kind a wife would..." He pulls the collar of his T-shirt away from his neck like it's strangling him.

"So go on dates! Oh my God. You can't hire a wife so you can get laid." I slap my hand over my mouth. That might have been a bit loud. And I can't believe I'm talking to Boone about getting laid.

"I don't have time to date." He's reading over his ad. "It doesn't have to be perfect. It just has to work."

"You sound like you're shopping for a car, not finding a wife. What about love?"

He shakes his head. "What about it? I don't need love. I need my house to be a home again. I need a partner. The bank says a loan would be easier to get if I was settled, too. Even though it wasn't my fault that I went...away...they say it would look better if I had a wife. Stability." He's looking across the street at the hardware store. "I have to catch up. I missed too much. I don't have time to...date. I just need to get started."

That's when I see what he's looking at. Amy Bennett...well, Amy Jones now. She's across the street pushing a stroller and rubbing her big belly. Amy used to be his girlfriend. She was the female Boone. Cheer captain, homecoming queen, and if I remember right, she was real smart, too. The whole blonde package.

And she married someone else when he was in prison. That's what he wants to catch up to. "Boone, you can't hire a wife. That won't get you what you want." I put my hand on his shoulder. "Just like I can't hire a decent childhood on Craigslist, you can't hire someone to erase the last five years. You need to do it the long way. Find a girl. Date. Fall in love. Then you can get married and have babies."

His jaw is so square I could play Tic-Tac-Toe on it. Every muscle in his body is tense. "Look at me. You think anyone in this town is going to want to go out with a newly released felon like me?"

"You aren't a felon!"

"Look. At. Me." I am. I do. All the time. Boone Barker used to set my girlish heart aflutter, but the huge slab of man in the booth turns my grown-up knees to jelly. He's massive and rough and virile. That wary look in his eyes never goes away and makes him seem almost feral. And he's looking at me now. No, he's looking through me. Like he can see how fast my heart beats for him.

Count it off. Three. Two. One. Speak. "I'm looking at you, and I still don't think you should hire a wife from Craigslist."

"Madeliiiine!"

I roll my eyes at the kitchen. "I have to go. Just...don't place that ad yet."

I push through the kitchen door and run right into Jay the dishwasher. The whole stack of plates flies out of his hands and crashes to the floor.

"Whoops."

Big Mac is beet red. The spatula in his hand looks like a weapon right now. He's either going to kill me or have a heart attack. "Madeline. For the love of...you are the clumsiest, most worthless waitress I've ever seen. I don't care what Vera says. I'm done."

Shit. No. "I'm sorry, Big Mac. Please don't fire me. I'll...pay you back for the plates." Somehow. I follow him toward the office even though I should let him cool down. "I'll work extra shifts. Please. You can't fire me. I don't have anywhere else to go."

He points at me, about to let loose a tirade of epic proportions and then stops. I turn to see what has him so bug-eyed to find an angry, hulking beast standing in the doorway separating the dining area from the kitchen.

Boone.

"You don't talk to her like that ever again." His voice is a low rumble, but no one could mistake his intent.

Oh, no. "Boone, please. Don't make it worse. I deserve it. I broke the..."

I don't get the rest out because he's stalking toward us, a grim determination on his face. His big, muscular forearms are flexing, and I realize it's because he's making fists. I rush between him and Big Mac. "Don't. I don't want to be the reason you do this."

What he doesn't need is to get arrested for assault. Not defending my honor.

"Nobody treats you like that. Not ever again," he says, his words a thick, low rumble. And then I'm in his arms, and he's carrying me back out of the kitchen like a groom carries a bride across the threshold.

"Boone!'

Marion is chasing us, only she's not trying to stop him. She's ...got my purse and hoody. She gets in front of him and stuffs my things into my arm and waves. "This is just like *Officer and a Gentleman*. Good luck, Madeline!"

"Good luck? Marion, help me. Boone, put me down!"

He grunts.

God, he smells good. It's not cologne. It's probably hay and diesel for all I know, but it packs a punch to all my girl parts.

And now we're in the parking lot.

This is crazy. I mean, if I were the kind of girl who kept a journal, I would totally write about this as being the most romantic thing that ever happened to me, but that doesn't mean it isn't nuts. "Boone! What are you doing?"

"Can you cook?"

"What?"

"Can you cook?"

"Yes. I mean…not like chicken cordon bleu or anything, but I can do the simple things. Why?" We're at his truck. "Wait a minute."

"Can you clean?"

"You are being ridiculous. I need to go back there and beg for my job back. Put me down. Why are you doing this? I mean, thank you for standing up for me. Nobody has ever done that before. But still, I need to go back."

"I need someone to cook and clean and keep my dad company and maybe plant some flowers. You need a job and a place to stay." He looks less angry, so that's a good thing.

"What happened to Craigslist?"

"This is better." He deposits me in the front seat of his truck.

"So, you're not going to hire a wife? You're going to hire me instead?"

"I'm going to marry you instead."

What?!

He closes my door and rounds the front end of his truck. I should open my door. Get out. He's not stopping me. But…I can't do anything but hear the words *I'm going to marry you.*

When he gets in, I ask, "You want to marry me."

"Yep."

"No."

"No?"

"No."

He puts the key in the ignition, but waits to start his truck. "Why not? You got a better offer? You'd rather work for an asshole who doesn't pay you and yells at you and calls you names in a job you hate?"

I'm pretty sure this is all a dream. This can't be my real life. "You're going to *pay* me to be your wife?"

"Well, no. But I won't yell at you or call you names."

My heart is racing like I'm the one who picked up a nearly two-hundred-pound girl and strode across the parking lot. "No, this is ...no. I can't marry you."

He starts the truck and he's whistling "The Farmer in the Dell."

"Boone. We don't even know each other. We can't get married. We're not in love."

Again, I'm not throwing open my door and jumping out. We're not moving yet. I still could.

"I figure we'll probably get there someday. But I don't think it's the most important thing."

I'm not sure which one to unpack first. That he thinks we'll fall in love someday or that he doesn't think love matters in a marriage.

"I can hear all your wheels turning. So, let me clear this up for you. We've both had some shitty luck, no one can say different. But we're still here. Still fighting, trying to make something of our lives. That makes us different from a lot of people. We're fighters, Madeline. Wouldn't it be nice not to have to fight alone for a change?"

Once I figured out that my upbringing wasn't normal, that there were different kinds of families, all I ever wanted was the kind I didn't have. The kind my father could never give me and certainly not the kind I found in foster homes. I may come off as pragmatic most of the time, but deep down, what I want is what he's offering. Only I want it to be real. "Marriage is a big deal."

"You think I don't know that? My folks were partners in every way. They never gave up on anything, but especially not each other. That's what I want. For me. For my kids."

"They loved each other, though. And I'm glad you had such a great model couple to watch, but I didn't. I don't know anything about a healthy relationship." An ache inside me blooms, knowing the truth and saying it are two different things. "I'm not the girl you are looking for, Boone. I wish I was, though. I wish a lot of things."

He reaches across the gearshift and grabs my hand. "You don't need to wish anymore. I think we want the same things. Let's just make them happen."

"How do you know what I want?"

"You think I don't see the way you look at me?"

Oh God. My face is burning hotter than the sun. "Boone..."

"I haven't been with a woman in five years, Madeline. Do you know who I dream about at night? Who I think about when I come in my hand?" He strokes my palm with his thumb. "You, sunshine. Ever since I came in the diner this spring, it's been you. And I've been trying to get past it. Trying to put you out of my head—even trying to take steps to find someone who isn't you to be my partner. Because you're too young and you've already had a hard life, I should leave you be. The last thing you need is to be attached to another man this town gossips about. But I can't stay away. I can't. And when that asshole was yelling at you, I knew it was useless to try."

If I were to sit down next to eleven-year-old Maddy Mae and tell her that Boone Barker, the quarterback who just threw the winning touchdown, would someday burst through the door, yell at her boss, and carry her out, pleading with her to marry him—she'd have passed out. Present day Maddy Mae is pretty close to fainting as well. This is just not my life. Men like Boone—especially the man he is now—are not interested in girls like me.

My hand looks so small in his.

"Are you admiring my nice hands right now?" he asks as he gives mine a squeeze.

I start to giggle. I can't help it. This whole situation is so totally weird. I look over at him and he's smiling at me. I haven't seen him smile, not like this. Big and real and happy. It transforms his whole face.

"Boone," I begin. "I'm not going to marry you and cook your meals and clean your house and make centerpieces for your table."

His smile falls, and his face is hard again.

"You said you wanted a partner." I take a deep breath. This is crazy. "This is the 21st century. We split the cooking and cleaning and decorating. And I help you with the chores and the planting and everything else."

It takes a few seconds for his face to catch up with his brain. "You're serious?"

"And I want to finish school. I can go part-time and do some of my classes online, but I want to finish."

"Absolutely."

I don't really see how this ends well. He'll figure out that I'm not good at anything. He'll realize that he could have planned better. Hell, even Craigslist might have gotten him a more suitable partner. But I'm so tired of always looking in the window of other people's lives and wondering why I can't ever get close to having that.

Boone is a good man. He's had more misfortune than a lot of people, but he's still showing up at life. Still trying to make the best of it. Fix what's wrong. I'm not going to pretend he's perfect—I'm sure prison messed him up a lot more than he shows—but his character still shines through.

And it doesn't hurt that he is hot as fuck.

"Madeline..." He draws my gaze back to his face. "I want a family. I'll want to start on that right away."

A family. Kids. Sex. Sex with Boone. Oh my God.

"Man, most guys don't even want to commit to a second date, and you want to talk about getting me pregnant before we've even kissed."

He pulls me half over the seat and presses his lips to mine. His hand delves into my hair and he tips my head back, angling me so he can go deeper. I open my mouth and his tongue slips inside. The rough groan he makes causes my nipples to tighten deliciously. His tongue rubs against mine, and I feel it like he's touching my pussy even though he's nowhere near it.

His kiss is everything.

He pulls back a bit. "The idea of getting you pregnant makes me harder than I've ever been in my life." He kisses me again, lighter this time. "But please don't ever talk about other guys again. It makes me crazy and my anger isn't as easy to control as it used to be. I'm feeling like a possessive asshole right now." He puts his big hand on my stomach. I want to suck it in. It's too soft. Too big. "I'm going to put a baby in you and then everyone will know you're mine."

I'm sure it's just biology, the reason that statement was so hot. But I swear to God, I just ovulated from his words. He wants to put a baby in me. My panties are soaked.

I need him to understand he doesn't have to get possessive though.

"Boone," I try to dislodge his hand, but he won't budge, "You don't need to worry about my past. I've never...you'll be my first."

Those green eyes darken as they dilate. "Not another word."

Oh shit. That was the wrong thing to say. "Are you...mad?"

Of course he is. That was the dumbest thing to tell him. He's been celibate for five years now. He's not going to want an inexperienced girl in his bed. He needs a real woman. A woman who knows how to please him. How to make up for all the years he's lost.

I think I just lost him and I barely had him. I'm so stupid. I try pushing his hand off my fleshy stomach. I don't need the reminder of my physical imperfections right now.

Instead of moving off me, though, Boone spans his fingers wide like he wants as much of me touching his hand as possible. "Mad?" he asks. "I'm on the razor's edge here, baby. It's been five years for me. You're telling me I'm going to take your virginity and knock you up at the same time, and I'm trying really hard to not rip your clothes off and do it right the fuck now." He leans his head back. "First, I'm going to marry you. Then, I'm going to make you come all over my cock. Then

I'm going to fuck my baby into you. That's the order. We need to go now."

"Where?"

"Idaho."

"Idaho? Wait, you want to get married today?"

"Right the fuck now."

Chapter Three

Boone

Someday, I will make it up to her. I know girls dream about their wedding day. Big white dresses and fairy tale endings. Hell, Amy had a whole three-ring binder devoted to her wedding day. That thing used to scare the shit out of me.

And what do I give my bride?

A courthouse. A judge. Two signatures. I don't even have a ring. She's wearing jeans and a diner shirt.

It's just that Idaho has no waiting period after applying for a license. And I'm tired of waiting. Living on the state border, it's what a lot of people do. People who'd rather *be* married than *get* married. But now that it's done and we're walking to my truck like we just went in and paid a traffic fine, not changed our entire lives, I wonder if I did the right thing.

She's exactly what I want. What I have wanted since I met her. But am I enough for her?

I guess I'll just have to make sure I do whatever I need to do to be what she needs. What she wants.

I will be the best fucking husband she ever dreamed about. I'll make a life for her. She looks a little wary right now, but I'll do it. I'll make her happy. She'll never be yelled at by an asshole again. She'll never have to flinch when someone calls her name. All the shit she's put up with for the last twenty years is over. And if she doesn't know that yet, she will. I'll show her every day.

We don't need to be in love. We just both need to want this to work. And I want this to work. I don't know what it is about her, but she means freedom to me—more than even my first step out of prison did.

Maybe I should try and explain that to her. Maybe if she understood...

I stop her on the bottom step of the courthouse. "Madeline?"

She blinks up at me. Those gray eyes assessing me carefully. She doesn't trust easily, that she's given me the benefit of doubt this much is a miracle.

"When I got out a few months ago...it didn't feel real. I was afraid to look around, look behind me. Like they were going to drag me back or worse, that it was a dream. I didn't feel free. I felt like I was dragging chains behind me. Chains that no one else could see. When you said, "I do," I finally feel like the shackles came off."

She gets this pinch of skin above her nose. Like there's math she's trying to do in her head. Then she stands on her tiptoes and kisses my cheek. "I'm afraid of waking up, too."

"Do you want to get some food? Or go home? Maybe go grab some stuff from your apartment?"

"That all sounds...fine."

Hell. She deserves better than this.

"No, it doesn't. Come on." I pull her with me to the truck. "I know the perfect place."

About ten minutes away from downtown, we pull into a casino resort. It's not five star, but it's the nicest place around. And I bet they have honeymoon suites.

She cranes her neck to look at the sign. "Boone, you know I'm not twenty-one, right? I can't gamble in the lounge."

"We're not going to the lounge."

At the front desk, I check us in to their best room—the clerk gives us an upgrade when she figures out we just got married. We don't have any luggage, but my new bride reluctantly allows me to buy her some things from the gift shop to change into. "I want you out of that damn shirt."

Her eyes widen.

Could I sound any more caveman?

"Not like that." Though, yeah, I'd love to see her out of the shirt and completely naked for me. "That shirt is a reminder of how pissed off I am. It makes me angry every time I think about the way Mac talks to you. The way you were supposed to feel grateful that they weren't paying you. You deserve so much more than that."

She shrugs. I don't try to argue with her about it. It's just going to take time until she realizes her worth.

When we get upstairs and into our suite, her eyes get bigger. "Oh my God!" She twirls around the room like I just took her to the Ritz. "Is this for real?"

I set down our shopping bags. "It's not that nice."

"Are you serious? This is the nicest room I've ever been in."

I didn't grow up rich by any means, but we always had more than enough. My parents took me to plenty of nice places. Family vacations were a regular thing. I can't wait to take my kids to Disneyland. My mom loved *Beauty and the Beast* so much.

"I'm glad you like it. It's supposed to be a really nice hotel."

She stops twirling. "Boone—I don't mean it's the nicest hotel room I've ever been in. I mean room in general. I've never been in a nicer room."

Madeline puts a lot of things in perspective for me. I had five years of a shitty existence—but she's had more than that. Nobody has ever treated her right. Not ever.

But I will.

"We're going to fix up the farmhouse. Even nicer than this. You're going to love it, I promise." My mom kept it up really well, but I know a lot of it is dated. The appliances could all be replaced, and my dad's den still has shag carpet in it.

She smiles at me. "I'm not worried." But her smile wobbles a little. "I'm not going to lie. I'm a little nervous about...everything."

Yeah, she's not talking about decorating our house. My sweet little virgin is remembering we're going to have sex in this room.

My heart pounds. I'm going to claim her. Make her mine. I can't fucking wait. But first she needs to relax. We both do. "I'm nervous, too, if that makes you feel better."

She's walking around the room, touching furniture. "You? Big bad Boone?" She stops in front of me. "Why are you nervous?"

"It's hard for me to remember how to not be an inmate. I want to show you the guy I really am tonight...but what if he's gone and all that's left is..."

She puts her hand on my heart. "Tonight, let's not worry about who we used to be. Fresh start?"

I nod and hold her hand there. It feels nice. "But you have to promise to tell me if I scare you or I'm acting...wrong."

"There is no right or wrong. I trust you, Boone."

She trusts me. No pressure.

Fuck.

"Are you hungry?"

She shakes her head. "Can I take a bath? I feel..." she gestures to her work clothes.

"Of course. Take as long as you need." The tub is big enough for two, but I figure she needs some time alone. Hopefully, she won't do so much thinking that she realizes this was a mistake on her part.

I order up some room service while she's in there. I pace while I wait, trying not to think of Madeline soapy and wet and naked just on the other side of the door.

I want to get started on making a baby. I want to get laid. But I can't push her too fast. She's a virgin. And this situation is crazy.

But knowing she's mine and only mine, well, it's hard to get my dick to stand down. I might need to go slow. Slower than I want to. Her first time should be good, though. About her, not me.

My dick disagrees, of course.

She comes out of the bathroom in a hotel robe shortly after the food arrives. I pour her a glass of champagne and try to think of something to say that doesn't sound cheesy when she touches my arm. "This is really nice. You're going through a lot of trouble for me."

"All I did was make a phone call to the kitchen."

Madeline shakes her head. "You're trying to make this special for me. And I appreciate it. I don't think I can eat right now. And I shouldn't drink...could you...hold me? Please?" She blushes and looks away. "I'm nervous."

She's nervous and she wants me to hold her. The last chain breaks for me. My woman, my wife, needs comfort and she wants it from me. I could never tell her in words what that means, how she just changed my life by asking for me. So, I pull her into my arms.

She's so soft. I want to sink into her. I hope I'm not holding her too tight. "Madeline, whatever you need. From now on, you get whatever you need."

She sighs and melts into me. "I feel like a princess. You're going to spoil me." She presses deeper, and there's no way she can't feel my iron-hard cock. She doesn't pull away, though. Instead, she makes this tiny groan and rubs against me.

"I want to spoil you." And I do. "If you keep doing that—"

"The things you said to me in the truck. About a baby..."

"If you're not ready tonight—"

Her hand grabs my rod through my jeans. "It made me really hot."

My world pinpoints to one thing. "It did?"

She nods. "It so did."

I'm a smart man. You don't need to tell me twice to talk dirty to my wife.

"Jesus Christ, baby. I'm going to love knocking you up." I take her hand off my pants so I don't come in them right now. "I'm going to lay you on that bed and get that sweet pussy on my fingers and tongue. I can't wait to taste you."

"That won't make a baby..."

"Don't you worry about that. We've got plenty of time for you to come all over me before I even take my cock out."

I swoop her up and take her to the bed. I untie the sash on the robe and spread it open so I can see all her womanly curves. My mouth is watering. "You're beautiful." She tilts her head away, so I direct her chin back toward me. "I don't lie. I'll never lie to you. Never. You're beautiful. Your body is beautiful. It's ripe and round and ready for me to plant my seed." I run my hands down her skin, over her ample hips and silken thighs. "So lush. You're a dream. I've come so many times thinking about you. I can't believe you're really here."

"When you say those things to me...I want to believe you."

"You felt how hard I was. You know how much I want you."

I push her legs apart gently. Her pubic hair is glistening. Fuck. She's wet. So wet. My mouth is watering. I run my thumb gently through her slit and she bucks her hips. I can't wait until she's bucking underneath me, but we'll take our time right now. I bring my thumb to my nose, inhale her sweet scent, and then lick the juices. "So sweet."

She ignores my comment. "You still have all your clothes on."

"Yeah. I'm keeping them on for now. Once I take my dick out, I don't think I'll be able to control myself, and I want to savor you from head to toe.

She pinkens, the color crawling down her face to her chest. Her tits are going to be my new religion—so much better than even my imagination. I take the globes in hand and they spill out, generous and full. Her eyes close and she arches into my hold. "You're perfect. Look at you." I take one berried nip in my mouth, and she gasps as I suck it hard. "You like that, sunshine?" I do it again, this time to the other.

I'm going to fuck those tits. I've dreamed about it. I want to oil them up and slide my dick between them. I want to cover them with my come. Not until I know she's pregnant, though. I won't waste a drop of come anywhere but inside that pussy until I know she's bred.

She grasps the back of my head and holds me to her chest. The feral noise I make should scare her, but it doesn't, and I nurse on her, sucking and biting as much of her into my mouth as I can. The way she's bucking and arching is frenzied, out of control. I palm her juicy pussy with one hand, and she grinds into my palm. She might be untried, but my little virgin is into what we're doing.

I move down her body, my stubble scraping across that soft belly. I place a kiss there, knowing the gift she'll give me someday. "Mmmm, you've got the perfect belly for babies. It's going to be so beautiful, so hot swelling with my child."

"Oh, God. Boone—"

When I get my face near her perfect pussy, she tenses up. I breathe her in, rubbing my nose gently against the curly hair between her legs. I part her pussy lips with my tongue, lavishing her with a long, slow lick. The sweet, smooth flesh is glistening with her pleasure. Pleasure I'm giving her. I've never felt more like a real man.

My dick is leaking in my pants. *Patience, asshole.*

I rub the flat of my tongue over her clit repeatedly. Broad strokes over that sweet little pearl. Her legs tremble and my patience is snapping. I need inside her body. I need it now.

Fuck her with your tongue.

I spread those lips with my fingers and slide my tongue right into heaven. Her juices are dripping down my chin and she's crying out my name. Over and over. I'm lost in her. I'm dry humping the mattress, pushing the headboard into the wall and thrusting my tongue into her sweet flesh. She's drowning me, but I don't need air. Just Madeline. I just need Madeline.

Her whole body tenses and shudders violently as she comes hard, grinding on my face. I feel like a king. A god. It was worth every minute in that cell if she is my reward.

My cock is straining against my pants, aching to get out. To plunder her the way my tongue did.

"I think you killed me," she says, moaning. "That was the best way to go, though."

She rises up on her elbows and blushes.

"What is it?"

"Your face...it's..."

Soaked. My face is soaked. "And that embarrasses you?"

She nods. "Is that... am I normal?"

"Sunshine, nothing we do together in our bed will ever be wrong or abnormal. I love that you are so wet for me. I love the way you smell and taste and it turns me on."

"Really? You swear?"

"I told you I would never lie to you."

"Show me, then. Show me how turned on you are. I want to see you."

Madeline

HE WHIPS HIS SHIRT off and I'm mesmerized by the dips and valleys of his chest and abs. Of his tanned skin pulled tautly over sinewy muscles. He's a giant...a giant made of granite. So virile and strong. I can't believe I'm here with him. In bed. Married.

When he shucks his pants and underwear in one swoop, all I see now is the monster between his legs.

It looks...angry. Purple and veined and dripping. There is no way it's real. Below the glistening beast, his balls are gloriously heavy and large. Of course, he's big there. I just never realized how *big* big could look.

"That's it, sweetheart. Look at my cock. Your eyes are so big right now. It's making me harder." As if to punctuate his words, the monster twitches. "You don't need to be scared, though. Baby, you were meant for this cock. For the things I'm going to do to you. There's not a doubt in my mind you can take it. That you'll take it all and beg me to give it to you harder. I'm a lucky man. To be your first. Your only."

If he fits, sure. "How do you know...it looks so big."

He fists it, jacking it slow, and my pussy contracts around the hollow feeling inside me. I want to be filled. With him. But he'll cleave me in two with that thing.

"I was made for you. I was made to fit inside you. To fill you. To give you pleasure."

I want to believe him so badly. "Come hold me again?" I ask. And he's on the bed a second later, pulling me into his arms tightly. All the chatter in my head dies down as we spoon. His protective embrace holding my doubts at bay. I inhale deeply. I don't know if it's pheromones, but his scent affects me. Settles me. "I feel so safe right now."

"I'll always keep you safe."

I wiggle against his erection. God, there is no way that thing is going to fit inside me. But, no. He said it will and I choose to believe him. I trust him.

Oh my God. I trust him.

I've never trusted anyone before. Not really. I've always felt so alone.

I turn so we're facing each other. I want to please him. If I can give him even a little bit back of what he's given me. The way he makes me feel.

With both hands, I reach for his hard cock. It's velvety and heavy. As I move my hands up and down its length, Boone gasps, the tendons in his neck standing out as he grunts loudly.

"Easy, baby. You'll make me come too fast."

I meet his eyes. "And you want to come inside me."

"Yeah, I want to come in your pussy. So bad."

"And make a baby. Tonight?"

"I'm going to fuck a baby into you. Tonight. Is that what you want?"

I want to make up for all the things he's lost. Make him feel like he made the right choice making me his wife.

"Yes." I squeeze him, and he swears. "I want you to. Tonight. Now."

He rolls us over and lays his hard, weighty cock on my stomach, his plump balls rubbing on my mound. "I'm going to pump every drop right up inside your little cunt...my balls are aching and full right now. It's been so long, baby. I'm ...gonna drain them as deep as possible inside you." He's using his cock to massage my clit, and he's looking deeply into my eyes. "Once I get inside you, I won't let up until I flood you with my come. Is that what you want?"

I raise my hips so I can slide myself against him, his dick making a path between the lips of my sex. I'm so slick and hot and achy for him. "Yes. Yes. Please."

"Good girl." He pushes his fat cock into me slowly. It burns a bit, and I pull back instinctively, but I have nowhere to go. "Shh. Relax, sunshine. Let it happen. You want my baby in you, don't you?" I nod. "Take a deep breath."

He pushes in further, and I force myself to relax as he glides into me slowly, inch by inch. My pussy is wrapping around him, so wet. I'm full. Too full. I grasp his shoulders, and my nails sink into his skin.

"Breathe, Madeline." He holds still, and I know that must be torture for him. I stretch around him, feeling every quake and pulse of his cock deep inside me. "Oh fuck, baby, you're so fuckin' tight," he groans.

The stinging sensation lessens, and I look up, into his intense gaze. He's watching me so closely. His whole body is taut like elastic about to snap, but he's waiting. Waiting for me to be okay.

"Okay, more?" I say, framing his concerned face in my hands. "I'm ready."

"Are you sure?"

I nod.

He pulls back several inches then surges forward. The further into my tight pussy he goes, the more I want to feel him pulsing deep inside me. He's awakened something in me. Something instinctual. His cock feels so good in me, hard and hot and filling me up as he glides slowly at first, and then faster and harder. The pleasure is overwhelming, building. He's going to make me come again.

He has a good rhythm going now, sliding his cock in and out quickly, grinding up against my clit with every inward stroke. He kisses me passionately, desperately, before resting his face against my cheek, breathing hotly and moaning in my ear as he pumps into me. "You're everything I dreamed you were," he whispers.

I cling to him on every outward stroke, not wanting to be separated. I have a frantic need to be filled. I don't care if it's biology tricking me into feeling things that aren't true. He may not love me, but he married me. He wants to give me a baby. That's got to be enough, right?

He braces my knees back, thrusting in deep, and I feel his cock start to twitch and throb "Oh, yeah, baby, I can tell you like that. The way your pussy is squeezing me. You love me taking your pussy like this, don't you?"

"Yes!" I cry. "I didn't know it could be like this."

He uses one of his giant hands to gently swipe the hair off my face. "I didn't know either, sunshine. It's never been like this for me before either."

I don't question him. He told me he wouldn't lie to me. Something about the two of us together is different, better than anything else. I feel...special. And I feel something else. Something I never thought I'd feel. A special kind of peace I know I'll only find in his arms, in his bed, in his life.

"Madeline, I'm on the edge. I don't think I can hold out much longer. I want to fuck you all night, I swear, but I'm desperate to come right now."

A wave of womanly instinct crashes over me. I want him to come. I want to *make* him come—harder than he ever thought possible. "Look at me, Boone." He looks me in the eye. "Don't hold back. Make me yours. I've been waiting my whole life for you to make me your woman."

His nostrils flare. "Everyone is going to know you're mine when you're waddling around with my baby inside you, aren't they?"

I nod and his hands grip my ass so tight he's going to leave marks.

"Are you claiming me as your man, sunshine? They're all going to know. You sure? I can pull out. It'll kill me, but I can do it. For you. If you need more time."

I grasp his biceps tightly. "I'm proud to be your wife, Boone Barker. Come inside me. I need to feel you come."

There is an intimacy that emerges between us that is unlike anything I have ever felt. We connect on every possible level. Physically. Mentally. Emotionally. Spiritually. Like we are one. At that moment, he groans, and I feel his seed spurt into me in long, drawn-out pulses. My pussy contracts around him as I join his orgasm.

"God, you're milking it right out of me. I'm never leaving this fucking bed."

He doesn't pull out of me when he's done. He lays his head on my chest and rolls his hips, keeping a gentle rhythm that feels like an ancient heartbeat. He's getting thick again as he pushes his leaking seed back into me. We keep rocking and he starts sucking my breast until I arch and throb everywhere with another powerful orgasm.

"That's it. God, you're so beautiful. Going to make me come again."

We're sticky and messy, and by the end of the night, I don't think there's a chance we didn't make a baby.

Chapter Four

Boone

It feels like we had sex more last night than I would have in the last five years combined if I'd been free.

My dick aches. I've got scratches up and down my back from Madeline's fingernails. Every muscle I have is sore, and I can't drink enough water today.

Life is fucking good.

I look over at my wife snoozing in the passenger seat. She looks well-fucked and fertile. I want her again, despite knowing it's probably physically impossible for me to ejaculate another time today.

But she's got to be sore. I pounded that poor pussy of hers too hard, too many times. Not one complaint from her though. Not one.

Now I'm getting hard. Her plump body, her juicy pussy, her enthusiasm for everything we did last night was more than a dream come true for me. We hardly know each other, but she's taking a chance on me. She's believing in me the way few people did when the chips were down. I knew I liked her—but it's more now. I have a strong sense of loyalty to her, but more than that, I feel like maybe we're meant to be.

If you'd have told me two months ago I'd live to see the day that I didn't believe that Amy was the woman for me, I'd have never believed it. I don't blame Amy for carrying on with her life. I'd have told her to do it if she'd ever come to see me. But I thought I would mourn that lost love for the rest of my life.

I guess I don't know how my little Madeline would have reacted if she'd been my girl five years ago. But something tells me, something I feel bone-deep, that she'd have stood by me. That she'll stand by me for the rest of our days. All I have to do is believe in her the way she believes in me.

It's not easy to trust. But I know if I treat her like she might betray me at any time, I'll be setting myself up for failure. I need to put all my efforts into making this marriage work. That means trusting her. That means treating her like a queen. That means my life suddenly feels limitless again. Like it did when I graduated from the university.

One night changed my life back then. One night just put me on a better path today.

We pull into the backside of Big Mac's where she told me she lived. "Hey, sunshine."

She blinks awake and sits up like the seat just burned her ass. "Why are we here?"

Her voice is tight, and my protective instincts rise. "Hey, it's okay."

She bites her lip then turns her head away from me. "I should have known. I'm so stupid."

"Known what, sweetheart?"

"It's okay, Boone. I'll be fine."

"Baby, what are you talking about?"

"You changed your mind. You're leaving me here. I mean, I get it. It was a crazy night. I just...I just thought...you didn't even hint..."

I reach over and push her hair away from her face so I can look at her. Fuck me, she's crying. "Madeline, sweetheart. I'm not leaving you here." I unbuckle her seatbelt and then my own so I can slide across the bench seat and get an arm around her. "Why would you think I'm leaving you here? I thought you might want to pick up your things before we go home."

She does that little shudder thing that happens when you're trying to hold in a sob. "Home?"

I cradle her to my chest. "Home, honey. I swear. You don't ever have to worry about me leaving you. I'm fucking crazy about you."

"You are?"

"Insanely. You're stuck with this big oaf till death do us part, remember?"

She wipes tears onto her sleeve. "I just saw where we were and figured you came to your senses while I was napping."

I kiss her sweetly because she needs some sweetness. And so do I. "You and me. From now on, I promise. We face everything together and you never have to worry again about being left."

"You're a good man, Boone. I don't know what I did to deserve you, but I really thought I just woke up and discovered it was all a dream."

For five years, I've been cultivating meanness. I had to learn to leave that All-American kid I used to be in the past so I could get hard and cruel in order to survive. Now, I need to relearn tenderness. This sweet woman in my arms had a life of pain, and I need to show her something new. "My mom would have really loved you, Madeline. She'd be so happy I met a girl who could wrap me around her little finger so easily."

"I'm still not convinced this isn't a dream."

"Let's go get your stuff."

We climb rickety steps with at least one rotting board to get to her room. The door is a piece of shit with no deadbolt. The room we step into is musty. She's got it as clean as it can get, but my cell was homier than her lodgings. Anger bubbles inside me. It takes every ounce of control I have to not punch a hole in the wall and then go find Mac and punch a hole in his throat. God damn it. They didn't pay her wages so she could live in this shithole?

She looks around and shrinks visibly. "It's not very nice."

Now I understand why she was so excited about our suite last night.

Moving behind her, I lay my hands on her tense shoulders and rub them until she loosens up some. Pressing a kiss to her temple, I tell her, "You're going to have a home. A nice one. You'll be safe and happy there. I'll make sure of it."

She turns and presses her cheek to my chest. "I'm afraid to want it too badly, Boone. I've never let myself really want anything. My dad showed me how hopeless that was, and it didn't get better after he was gone."

"Did he hurt you?"

"Not like you're thinking. He didn't hit me. Hell, he couldn't bring himself to touch me. Said girls were sinful. That I was his cross to bear."

This woman is making it difficult for me to work on my anger management skills. "He was wrong. You're not a sin or a burden. You're this ray of sunshine that reminded me I could be human again. I'm going to take you home, Madeline. We're going to make a life."

She nods, but she's still unsure.

There isn't much she wants to take. Mostly school stuff and some clothes. We're putting the last of it in my truck when Big Mac comes barreling out of the back of the diner to us. I stand in front of her and cross my arms.

"Boone, step aside," he tells me.

"I don't think so. Go back to your diner and leave her alone."

He peers around me. "Are you okay, Madeline? He's not threatening you, is he?"

Before she can answer, I do. "You've got a lot of nerve."

"We don't always get along, but she's my responsibility. I won't have you intimidating or hurting her."

Part of me is pissed at the accusation, but another part is grateful that he even cares about her that much. "I'm taking her out of this dump, and she's done working for you for free."

She steps around so she's not behind me anymore. "I'm fine, Mac. Boone isn't hurting me or intimidating me."

"Madeline, I know I don't always say nice things to you, but you know Vera and I don't want bad things to happen to you. Are you sure you're okay?"

I put my arm around her. "My wife is fine. You sure you're not just pissed about losing your free labor?"

"Wife?" he says, his face turning purple. "You got married?"

"Yesterday," Madeline says.

"Madeline, he's just out of prison. He's..."

"He's my husband."

Pride fills my chest. Heaven knows how much I've enjoyed saying "my wife" the last twenty-four hours. But hearing "my husband" from her lips shoots me to a new high.

Mac points at me. "You were a good kid and what happened to you was bad. But if you think marrying this young girl is going to fix it all, you're not being realistic. And you're just going to hurt her. What's more...I've known your dad a lot of years, son. What do you think he's going to say about this?"

"My dad is going to love Madeline."

Mac shakes his head. "Good luck with that. You're going to need it."

Madeline

WHEN WE'D BEEN PACKING up the truck, I was excited about starting fresh at the farm. But now, as I walk up the front steps, I keep hearing Mac's words in my head like a warning.

What if Boone's dad doesn't like me? What if he convinces Boone that his impulsive, rash decision to marry the girl from the diner was a mistake? What if they kick me out?

The house seems sad. Not sad like my horrible apartment sad. More like...it used to be happy and now it's grieving. As we walk in, I can imagine it bathed in sunlight and awake with fresh air instead of shuttered up like only ghosts live here.

The wall of pictures stops me and my heart races, realizing that I've married Boone Barker! That everyone, including his dad, is going to think that I tricked him into it. Maybe I did? I mean, obviously, it was his idea. But maybe I was preying on him because he was weak and needy, fresh out of prison and missing the woman he was supposed to marry.

"You okay?" he asks me.

"Maybe we should have dated a few times. Like normal people. We don't have to tell your dad yet. We can just be friends."

"My dad is going to love you." He reaches for my hand. "Is this about what Big Mac said? Are you having second thoughts?"

"Not about me."

His face registers surprise.

"This is like a fairy tale for me, Boone. You swooped in and literally swept me off my feet and offered me a home and a family and orgasms. But what do you get?"

"A home and a family and orgasms," he replies.

I almost laugh. Almost. "You can do so much better than me. You know you can. Boone, things are hard right now because you just got back. But you know everyone is going to come around. And you know women will be throwing themselves at you. And then you're stuck with a woman you don't even love and a forever you don't want."

His jaw squares and he's trying to hold in feelings. "Give me one month."

"One month?"

"Give me one month to show you this is going to work. If you still have doubts...well, I probably won't let you go very easily, but we can at least discuss it then. But you give us thirty days and you go all in. You try as hard as you can to make it work and I'll do the same and we'll have a date in one month and decide if we can continue."

"So we're just planning to be married for a month and then we see how it goes?"

"I already know how it's going to go. I just need to prove it to you. I'm not stupid. I saw how upset you were when you thought I was taking you back to the diner for good. But I also know you've had a shortage of people in your corner. You're going to need more than just me saying words to show you that you're not alone anymore. That it's okay to invest in a dream." He brings my hand to his lips and presses a tender kiss to it. "But you can't hold back thinking the deadline is coming. You have to be brave and give yourself to this marriage like you mean it."

"And the baby you're hoping to make? What if you decide at the end of our trial marriage that you want out and I'm pregnant by then?"

"Are you afraid I won't take care of you and my child?"

"Of course not. I know you'll do right by us. But Boone, it's a big complication. We should wait to conceive." His eyes get big. "I know you've been celibate for five years. I'm not saying we shouldn't have sex. I'm saying we should use protection. Try not to get pregnant."

"That's not going all in, sunshine. You can't trust me a little bit, you have to trust me completely."

"It's the responsible thing to do."

He shakes his head. "No, it's not. I'm not wearing a condom with you. Ever. We just don't have sex for thirty days. Until you're sure of me, of us, we don't fuck."

Chapter Five

Boone

One week later

I'm the stupidest man alive. I had the best sex of my life a week ago, and I voluntarily put myself on a fast.

Other than sleeping in the room *next door* to my wife every night, married life is good. I've just been out working on the tractor, and I've come in for supper. I walk past the den where my dad is snoozing with a game on. Something he still does too much of. I step into the kitchen and find my wife bent over as she empties a dustpan.

I'm celibate, but I'm not dead. I grunt to let her know I'm there right before I grab a handful of that ass and squeeze. "Kitchen looks good."

Since she's not much for repairing machinery, she offered to do a deep cleaning of the kitchen while I worked in the shop. Every morning, we have breakfast together and discuss what we want to get done—either separately or together. We divide and conquer chores, or we finish them together. She's my partner in everything. She's informed me I need to not be sexist about "women's work" and she's right.

Also, I'm completely in love with my wife.

I can't believe it myself. I knew I liked her. I knew I wanted her. I didn't know how fast or how hard I would fall. It's deeper than my feelings for Amy ever were. I don't understand that either. I've known Amy most of my life. When we started dating, it seemed like everything was as it should be. I didn't know I could feel more than I did. It's like Madeline opened up a new section of my heart, one that I didn't know existed. One that was made only for her.

She holds on to her reservations, but I have a gut feeling she loves me too. It's still twenty-one days until I get back in that sweet pussy, but I have some ideas about that.

I told her I won't wear a condom, and she told me she's not ready to get pregnant. This past week, we've still been affectionate, but not sexual. I'm thinking that there was nothing in our agreement that states we can't get each other off without risking pregnancy. And I'm aiming at seducing my wife. Tonight.

She turns in my arms and loops her wrists around my neck. "Hello there."

I slide my hands down to her hips and my desire for her sings in my blood as I pull her into my erection and take her mouth with slow, drugging kisses. She whimpers helplessly into my mouth and presses into me as hard as she can. Good. Nice to know I'm not the only one affected.

"Supper smells good." I'm hungry for something else though.

"I fed Pops about half an hour ago. He's a little grumpy about leaving tomorrow, but I think he's still on board."

"I don't know how you convinced him to go to rehab. I couldn't even get him to admit he was drinking too much."

She runs her fingers through my hair, moving it out of my eyes tenderly. "He didn't want to burden you with more problems. Once I got him to talk about your mom, he admitted she'd hate the way he's become. He wants to make her proud. And you."

I grab her hand so I can kiss her fingers. "I think it's you he wants to make proud. Ever since we told him we were married, he seems to have perked up."

She giggles. "Yes, he asks me about grandchildren every day. I...haven't told him we sleep in separate rooms upstairs. That we're doing a trial run."

I squeeze her hand. "It's not a temporary marriage, Maddy Mae. Just a temporary hold on making babies. There is nothing *trial* about this for me. You know that right? I'm more sure of us every day."

"Thank you for being so patient with me." She's scared, I can see it in her eyes. Not afraid of me, but afraid of letting herself get too comfortable, too sure of her footing. If you don't want too much, you can't get hurt when it disappears. But every day, I can see her walls crumble a little. "It's my job to take care of you and make you feel safe and happy. I have all the patience in the world for you."

She bumps into my erection and raises her brows. "Not all of you is patient."

"Yeah, well, you're fucking sexy. I want you all the time. Besides, I've been thinking..." Her face falls. "Relax. I'm not changing the terms."

"Sorry...what were you thinking?"

"I want to make you come, again."

Her face registers shock. "You just said..."

I cup her face in my hands and dip down for a long, slow kiss. "Making you come won't get you pregnant. I want to be close to you, like we were on our wedding night. But we don't have to have that kind of sex. I need to taste you, sunshine. And feel your skin. I want to hold you when you fall asleep and see you first thing in the morning. It's killing me to have a wall between us."

"Okay."

"Okay?"

She smiles at me like a woman who owns a man. "I want that too. I want that closeness. You know, if you would wear a condom—"

"Not happening. I want to fuck you more than I want anything else in the world, but not until you're ready for my baby."

"Well, I'm not."

"Then we find our pleasure other ways." I tuck the hair behind her ear. "There are a lot of other ways."

She blushes.

"Tonight then?"

"Tonight."

We eat supper, get Pops in bed, and sit down at the table to plan out some crop issues. She's come up with an idea we want to explore. Instead of commercial crops, we're looking at running a produce farm share program. It's not as profitable, in a lot of ways, but we're both concerned about sustainable crops and feeding the community fresh, whole food.

When I was a kid, we had a couple cows and chickens. It's been a long time since we had that kind of traditional farm on this land. But it feels right. We can rotate crops and have a bit of a pumpkin patch that families can come to. Since I graduated with an ag science degree and my wife is currently going to school for marketing, we've been brainstorming how to bring people to us. When they're here, drinking fresh cider and picking fresh pumpkins, we can interest them in contributing to the farm via a CSA program. We'd get their investment money before planting season, and they'd get fresh produce boxes every week during harvest.

It feels good to start this now. A way to mend my ties with the community. A new project for my wife and I to work on together.

But my brain is not on brainstorming. It's on getting her naked.

"Let's call it a night."

She inhales. "I'm suddenly nervous. Like I was our wedding night. Sometimes, I wonder if I dreamed it."

I think about the fact that she might already have my child growing in her, and my dick grows two sizes. "Not a dream. I'll prove it to you."

I take her hand and bring her to the room she's been staying in upstairs. It has a bigger bed, and I want room to play. Once I close the door behind us, I can't stop. I grab her, maybe too roughly, and drag her to the bed. My hand slides under the hem of her T-shirt. Her skin is warm and soft. A small mew escapes her throat, and I pull her to me more tightly. God, to hold her, it is more than enough and not enough at the same time. She burrows into my neck, and I soothe her with even strokes of my hand on her back while I inhale the scent of her hair as if it were air. Her body snug against my own.

Pressing my forehead to hers, I let out a slow breath.

I am going to show her everything I'm afraid to say tonight.

I take her mouth, crushing her to my body and kissing her fiercely. She whimpers and clutches my forearms while I take the words of surprise from her lips and replace them with a different need. My need for her that bites and twists, soothes and loves.

I bruise her with my mouth while I plunder her sweet lips, searching for what only she can give me. She emits a female sound of pleasure that goes from my ear straight to my cock. My hand on her belly moves up, cupping her bare breast while I deepen the kiss, groaning. Nothing should feel so good.

Her nipple tightens under my palm. It's perfect and I can't believe I deprived myself of her for a week.

She sucks on my tongue and I go cross-eyed with lust. I pull back so I can sit her up and get the damn shirt off her. I need to see those perfect tits. Need her skin with nothing between us.

"You're amazing," I tell her once she is bared to me. "Fucking amazing." Her breasts fill my hands, the rosy tips better than any dream. I bend to lick one and she arches, giving me all of her. Trusting me completely. So I draw the peak into my mouth, sucking while she gasps my name.

My fingers trace the skin of her stomach, circling her navel. She is lush—her skin and curves driving me mad with the silky heat. I kiss her there, right below her belly button where her skin is the softest. She doesn't try to get me away from her stomach this time. Hopefully it's because she finally believes me that I love it. I love the soft shape of her. That she's a cushion for the hard man I've become.

I can smell her, the light musk reaching into the most primitive parts of me. *Mine.* She's all I want.

I sit up and pull my own shirt off, proud when I see a feminine glint of appreciation light her eyes. "See something you like, sunshine?"

"Are you teasing me?" She pushes up onto her knees.

"I want to please you, baby. I need..."

She places a palm on my chest. "What do you need?" Both her hands wander over my chest and shoulders now. Her greedy hands stroke over me like she is afraid I am going to stop her. As if I don't like the sparks her fingertips leave in their wake. As if I'm not taut, every muscle tense, every nerve ending wishing for her touch.

Maybe I do need to stop her. I'm already too close, too on the edge. When she adds her hot mouth to her exploration, I groan and reach for her wrists. She continues using her mouth, stopping on a nipple, flicking it with her tongue. The answering pull inside me is like a powerful ocean tide on my control.

I have to push her back. I don't want to. But I don't want to end the show before I've even gotten my pants off. "Madeline."

"You didn't answer me." I bring her wrists behind her, so she leans forward, caressing me with just her breasts. "Tell me, Boone. Tell me what you need. Can I use my mouth? Will you show me how?"

Her words inflame me beyond all reason. The last hold I have on my control snaps as I use one hand to keep her wrists still and the other to snake into her yoga pants, grabbing her ass and pulling it to me. I squeeze the globe, the satisfying weight of it gives me even more ideas about what I want to do to her.

I want her bouncing on my cock, riding me. I want to taste her, make her writhe on my tongue. I want her beneath me, on top of me, on her knees, against a wall. I want her to swallow me, milk me dry with her mouth. I want to come in her ass while fingering her slick clit. I want to slide my dick between her lush breasts. Every dirty fantasy I've ever had—I want all at once.

As I squeeze her ass, I kiss her, trying to tell her with my body what I need because there are no words. I push her into my cock that's straining against my jeans, while my mouth devours hers.

I need everything. Everything she has. Everything she was. Everything she will be. I need her to need me as desperately as I crave her now. To be mindless and primitive. To forget who we were. The convict and the crazy man's daughter.

She strains against my rough hold. I have just enough control left in me to pull back, to see if she is in distress. I look into her eyes, afraid of what I might find there. Instead, the fire in her gaze amps up my desire even more.

Madeline

HE DOESN'T SAY A WORD. But he growls as he throws me down, yanking my yoga pants off my legs. Getting off the bed and making short work of his own pants.

He is a work of art, thick with muscles and heat. His cock is...well, now I know I didn't remember that incorrectly. He's really too big for a mere mortal. The wicked glint in his eyes tells me he knows he's big. Knows he's intimidating. Knows I can take it. That he's remembering how I took it so well before.

He palms himself in front of me, all male pride and wonderful lust. Oh God. He is thick. And beautiful.

I work up some courage. "If you need a hand, I'm happy to assist."

He shakes his head. "If you touch me right now, I'll embarrass us both." Something about his long, slow strokes down his cock makes my pussy quiver.

I'm questioning my no baby-making rule.

"So, you're going to stay over there, then?" I widen my legs, giving him what I hope is an enticing view.

"Sunshine, you don't play fair. Lay down. All the way now."

I do as he asks and feel the bed dip from his weight. Instead of settling over me, he stays to the side a bit. Honoring our pact. I feel him touching me, but not with his hands. With the cock he holds in his hand, he rests it on my breast. My stomach flips at the sight of it there. The way it feels when he uses it to glide across my nipple and back. Hard as iron, wrapped in silky soft skin, he rubs the moist tip of himself against the tight, pebbled peak of my nipple,

"So pretty," he murmurs, as entranced by the sight as I am.

It is more erotic than I expected. The ridge rubbing across my now diamond-hard nipple. He continues his exploration, gasping now and then as the sensitive underside of his dick strokes over my skin. He is marking me, claiming every inch of me with his thick, hard cock. It's primitive. A dark desire that should feel out of place in modern times, but doesn't.

I knot the quilt beneath me in my hands. I want to touch him. I want to taste him. But being owned by him is the hottest thing that has ever happened to me.

He straddles me, bringing that rigid cock to my cleavage and squeezing my breasts around his girth.

Okay, *this* is the hottest thing that has ever happened to me. He throws his head back like some sort of primal god, the cords of his neck straining with pleasure.

"Look at me, Boone."

He moves his hips again, hissing in pleasure, but continues to stare at the ceiling.

"Look at us." I put my hands over his, squeezing my flesh around him.

"If I look at you right now, I'll come. I have no control left. Not an ounce."

He rocks again, and I snake my tongue around his crown on the upstroke. He looks down at me then. Fierce passion scorching me, his nostrils flaring, his huge hands squeezing me hard enough to leave marks. "Madeline."

I love the salty taste of his pre-cum. I try to keep my lips around him longer each time he passes back up. Oh, this is hot. The look on his face. The feel of that fat cock on my tongue. My tits cushioning his shaft, but the crown is for my lips.

He stops thrusting, his body rigid and tight. We've only spent one night together, but I know when my man is ready to come. And he is ready.

"I want you to come. On me. All over me."

"I want to make it last, sunshine."

He thrusts and holds ten seconds longer when I get him in my mouth and suck. He pulls back, and I say, "We've got all night. Let yourself go. I want you to so badly, I want to be sticky and dirty and yours—"

He begins shaking, every corded muscle tense and defined, his eyes glazed over in lust. "I've dreamed about you like this," he says, a clear warning in his voice. "Dreamed of what you would look like if I painted you with—"

He doesn't finish his thought with words, but his orgasm tears out of him with a violent groan. He spends his come all over me, glazing my chest just as he promised, and I am shaking though I haven't come myself.

I'm close though.

I didn't know I could be so animalistic. Maybe some women would not appreciate being in my position right now, covered with sticky hot seed. But I revel in it. The dirtier the better.

"Is there a name for what we just did?"

He eyes me, blushing a little, which is sweet but unnecessary. "Sunshine, I'm..."

"Not sorry. Say it, Sunshine, I'm not sorry. Because I swear to God, Boone—"

"I treated you like a—"

"Woman you've been dying to fuck. To own. To claim."

"And that doesn't bother you?"

I raise up on my elbows, still sticky and hot. I look down my breasts, at the trails of jizz. "Not even a little bit." A look of tenderness crosses his face, so I send him a sassy smile. "What's it called?"

He shakes his head. "Titty fuck." He groans and rolls off me onto his back. "That doesn't sound very romantic."

I don't say anything, waiting for him to look at me. To see me rubbing him into my skin in circles with my fingers. His gaze darkens, and he swallows hard.

"I didn't look after your needs. Tonight was supposed to be about you."

"I enjoyed myself just fine."

He raises one brow. "I should have given you a hundred orgasms before I took one."

I lick his cream off my fingers. "I'm not going anywhere."

He growls and moves again, this time pushing my legs open. "You really did like that, didn't you?" He palms me between my legs, runs a finger over me where I ache the most. "So wet, sunshine." He continues to massage my clit, and I open my legs more. "Keep touching your tits. Just like that. God look at you."

I whimper as he brings his face down. Little shocks of electricity are running through my body as if I were a live wire.

"You're so pretty here. Your cunt is so wet and ready for me."

My pulse has settled between my legs like it's my new heart.

"Do you want me to make you come?" he asks.

"Yes."

He uses the tip of his tongue and very little pressure, a tickle almost. "Better ask nice, dirty girl."

"Please," I beg.

"Please what?" Another soft tickle and the scrape of his stubble on my inner thigh makes me squirm, but he tamps down my legs so I can't move. "Don't stop touching yourself and tell me what you want."

I pinch my nipples, and we both groan. "Please make me come, Boone. Use your mouth and make me come."

He hardly moves his jaw, just adds a little pressure, and I fall off the cliff chanting his name. He doesn't stop. He keeps at me, licking and sucking the area around my clit until I come down, and then he licks me there again, setting me off one more time.

I shake and my body quakes, knowing that pieces of me are cracked forever. I am broken. He's broken me.

"That's it, love," he says in that deep, rich voice that settles over my raw nerves like a blanket. "I've got you. Such a good girl."

I guess I went somewhere else. I have no idea how long I was gone, but I become aware that he is holding me, stroking my hair, telling me how good I am. How beautiful. And he kisses me, feeding himself back into me, filling the strange new cracks and making me feel whole again.

Chapter Six

Boone

One Week Later

I guess I knew it would happen eventually.

The last couple of months, I've seen glimpses of Amy and her family around town, but I haven't run into her. I've been dreading it. I'm not in love with her anymore, and I don't hate her. But part of me is still sore inside when I remember how she didn't believe in me. Didn't visit me once.

I feel trapped. Like the drugstore has morphed into my old cell. I want to pace the aisle like a tiger in a cage.

"Do you have a toothpaste preference? Boone?" Madeline nudges my arm. She's holding up two boxes. "Paste or gel? Earth to Boone..." She follows my gaze. "Oh."

Amy, my very pregnant ex-girlfriend, is headed directly toward us, pushing a cart with a child.

My head is buzzing. My hands clammy. This is it. The confrontation.

Amy stops near us and sends me a weak smile. She's still pretty, but looks a little tired. Pregnancy agrees with her, though. She has a glow. I hope that means she's happy. She exhales a huge breath. "Hi, I heard you were home. I wasn't sure if you wanted to hear from me, but I'm glad you're home."

My chest feels tight. "Thanks," I grind out and then take another breath. "You look...different."

She blushes, and her left hand goes to her round belly, her wedding ring catching the light. "Yeah, I...I'm a lot different than the girl you knew then, I guess." I count a hundred heartbeats off before she speaks again, looking down at her hand instead of looking me in the eye. "I like to think in addition to being rounder, I'm more mature than I was back...then...too." She bites her lip. "I was young and scared. I'm sorry. It's no excuse, Boone. You deserved better from me."

Now that the original zap of adrenaline has dissipated, I'm not feeling so intense. Maybe it's because I waited five years to hear those words. In my fantasies, she would make it up to me on her knees or sometimes she'd beg me to take her back and I would let her humiliate herself trying to make it up to me. Now, it's just closure. Closure I needed. "It's fine, Amy. It was a bad situation all around."

"I think I could have made it better, but didn't." She gets teary. She was never much of a crier in high school or college. But this situation is tense, and well, she's probably got pregnancy hormones adding to it. "I was really happy that they got the right guy. I..." She smiles a little at Madeline.

Shit. Madeline.

She's been quiet as a mouse and is trying to fade into the shelf behind her. I was too selfish to think how awkward this must be for her. "Baby, I'm sorry. This is Amy. She was my high school girlfriend." I look at Amy. "Amy, this is Madeline. She's my wife." A sense of pride fills me at the words.

Amy blinks a few times. "I...heard that rumor, but didn't believe it."

I put my arm around Madeline's waist and draw her into me. "Not a rumor."

She slinks out of my embrace. "I'm going to go pay for this and meet you at the truck. You two catch up. Nice to meet you, Amy."

I have no idea what that was all about.

"This is awkward, right?" Amy says. "Everyone says she's a nice girl, though. I'm happy if you're happy."

"I'm happy, Amy." I'm watching Madeline walk away until she turns the corner and I can't see her anymore.

"Right. It does seem strange though. You guys didn't know each other very long. I'm sure that she's feeling a little insecure right now. It's all very sudden, isn't it, Boone?"

I bring my gaze back to Amy. "I'm in love with her."

"Oh. Ohh." She smiles. "That's terrific then. I'm glad. Really."

It's a turning point for me, I guess. Seeing Amy and her beautiful little girl and her pretty pregnancy glow and ...not feeling like they should be mine. That they were ripped away from me. "I need to catch up to Madeline. Take care of yourself, Amy."

Madeline

The next day

I'M STARING AT THE pregnancy test I bought yesterday. I bought it in secret when Boone was in the aisle with Amy. He doesn't even know I suspect I'm pregnant. I don't think I can breathe.

In through the nose, out through the mouth, Maddy Mae.

I was so excited at first, when I missed my period. But seeing him with his ex-girlfriend made me remember that we still have two weeks. He might change his mind. He might realize that he should fight for his old life again. She's so pretty. What if what he really wants is Amy pregnant with *his* baby, and I'm just a poor man's substitute?

I hug myself around the middle and wait.

If I am pregnant, it's just barely. I only just lost my virginity and...oh my God. It's a plus sign. I swallow. Should I take the other test? Like a second opinion? Or should I wait a week and then take it. Give things a chance to...

Oh my God. Is this real?

I wrap the test in toilet paper and hide it in the back of my drawer, remembering how I used to squirrel away books so my father wouldn't find them.

If this marriage was real, I would go running out and find Boone and we'd celebrate. Instead, my first instinct is to hide it from him. He can't hurt me if he doesn't know where my weak spot is, right? I learned that from my dear old dad. He never knew that I had hopes or dreams or he would have crushed them just because he could.

Boone is not like that. I know he isn't. But I'm so afraid of wanting this marriage. This baby. This life. It's better, safer, to not care. Not want. Not need.

I have to get out of the bathroom. I have to just keep this to myself for now. For two weeks. If he changes his mind in two weeks, I won't tell him. I'll figure it out on my own. I've done it before by myself. Not well, but I managed. I throw open the door and run into the hall.

"You okay?" He's standing at the top of the stairs. "Madeline, you look pale. What's wrong?"

"I thought you were going to the feed store today?"

"I decided to wait until tomorrow. Have you been crying?"

I sniff loudly. "No."

"Madeline—"

Do I stand a chance competing against his past? Yet his past is all around us. Even now, in the hall, there's the room across the hall from ours that could threaten us. "You never go in this room." I point to the always closed door of his childhood bedroom. "Why?"

It's his turn to grow pale. "There's nothing I need in there."

"Are you so sure?"

"Madeline, what is this about?"

"Your past. It feels to me like you're holding on to it."

He shakes his head. "If I were holding on to it, wouldn't I be spending all my time in that room? Reliving my glory days. Maybe going to the bar every night and reminding everyone how I won that game. How I was the king. No, I'm not holding on to it. I put it firmly behind me."

"I think you won't go in there because then you'll remember what you're missing. What you want and don't have anymore. How you're settling."

"Settling? Maddy Mae, what has gotten into you? You've been acting weird since we ran into Amy yesterday. I told you. I'm not in love with her anymore."

There is this part of me that wants to revert to the old me. Go deep inside myself where nothing hurts. Where my father's tirades didn't affect me, and I didn't hear the snickers and taunts as people veered around us on the corner. Where I spent hours in a hard chair reading the bible, turning pages, but never really reading the words. Like I was watching myself. Never complaining to my father that chair hurt my bottom. That I was too young to be forced to read for hours. That I should bathe more often, eat more food.

That Madeline was as numb on the inside as her butt was on the outside.

But there is another part of me. The part that is so in love with Boone that I'd do anything to stay, even if he doesn't want me. I'd trap him with a pregnancy. I'd pretend we're okay even if we aren't. I'd lie to myself if I had to.

What I need to be is neither of those Madelines.

I need to be truthful. I need to be upfront. I need to say what bothers me and go after what makes me happy. Otherwise—my father wins. He tried to break me. I'm so tired of being broken.

"Boone, let's go in there. Together."

He shakes his head.

"Please. It's important to me."

He considers this for a long, tension-filled moment, and then he nods and opens the door.

For better or worse, we're going in.

Chapter Seven

Boone

It's freezing cold in my old bedroom. Which makes no sense since it's summer and hot as hell outside.

Madeline isn't shivering though, so it must just be me.

Nothing has changed since I moved to campus. I would only stay in this room during college breaks, so nothing has been done to it since I was in high school. It looks like a time capsule from the first decade of the millennium. My plaid curtains match the plaid bedspread. There are trophies on the shelves of all my accomplishments. Hell, there's even unopened mail on the desk. It's also dusty as fuck.

But there are no ghosts. Not like I thought there might be.

I sit on the bed and remember the time my dad came in with a beer and talked to me about sex while we shared a cold one. God, that was awkward. But necessary. He treated me like a man, and I wanted to be one worthy of him. I remember a dog name Misty who used to sleep at the foot of my bed. I remember a lot of things, but they don't hurt. I guess I'm doing better than I thought.

"How are you?" Madeline asks me.

"My mom would be pissed at the dust in here."

"Well, I hope she'd at least be happy with how the rest of the house is shaping up."

"She'd love you." I don't know what is going on in my wife's head. I thought that would make her happy, but she looks stricken.

"Did she love Amy?"

"Is that what this is about?" I hold my hand out to her and she takes it warily, joining me on the twin bed. "Yes, my mom loved Amy. We all did. She's a nice person. But she's my past. You're my present and my future."

"Your past is so much a part of everything. It feels like we are walking in two worlds everywhere we step in this house."

"Does it?" I look around. "I guess it's partly because I haven't faced it all the way. I keep trying to deny it. Like I'm not him, the kid that grew up in this room. That he died when I was arrested. But he's part of me, I guess. Part of us."

"Is he? He loved Amy...and I'm so different from her. I don't know if I'll ever believe..."

"Madeline," I cup her jaw and make her look at me, "I love you."

She inhales a shocked breath.

"I've been waiting for the right time to tell you. Now I see you needed the words sooner, and I'm sorry. I love you. I love that you are so brave and took a chance on me. I love that you call me on my bullshit. I love that you sit with me every morning and plan our life. That you make me face," I look around the room again, "you make me face my demons, but you are at my side when I do. You're the woman I want."

"I'm pregnant."

She's watching my expression so carefully, so I don't hide my smile. I don't know that I could. "You're sure?"

She nods. "I took a test. I wasn't going to tell you."

"What? Why?"

"Loving you scares me."

I feel like the sun is exploding warm light in my chest. "You love me?"

"Love is dangerous to me, Boone. It means being vulnerable. But I can't stop. And I'm so afraid of losing what we have that I'm afraid to keep it."

I slide to my knees in front of her. "You are my whole world. The only way you are going to lose me is if you leave me. But you'd take my heart with you. I love you. And I'll say it as many times as you need to hear it until you believe me."

"I love you too."

"So why are you crying?"

"I think because I'm happy. Boone, we're going to have a baby!"

I kiss her like my life depends on it. Because it does.

Thinking about her body swelling with my baby has me hard and ready to practice for the next one. "Baby, I've never had a girl in this room before," I tell her as I untie her shoes.

"Really?"

"Let's say we christen this bed."

"I'd be honored to be the first girl you have in this bed...but..."

Please don't let her doubt me still. "But what?"

"I think we should turn this room into a nursery. And it feels a little weird to get it on in our baby's room."

Holy fuck. We're having a baby. It just sinks all the way in and my vision tunnels.

"Boone? Are you okay?"

"I think I'm going to pass out."

"What? Why? Put your head between your knees."

I breathe through it and sit up again. My wife is laughing at me.

"You tell no one."

"Right. Who would believe me that Boone Barker fainted like a southern belle when he found out he was going to be a dad?" She's still laughing.

"I didn't faint. I almost fainted. And men call it passing out when they do it."

"Right. That's manlier." She snorts as she laughs. Which sets her off in another fit of giggles.

"That's it." I stand up and throw her over my shoulder like a fireman, swatting her ass as I carry her out of the room and into our shared bedroom. "I'll show you manly."

It occurs to me that now that she's pregnant, I can come in her and it won't be changing the terms of our deal. All the blood rushes to my dick.

Until I remember she might still think we're on a trial run. "Madeline," I slide her down my body, making sure she can feel how hard I am for her, "about the two weeks we have left…"

She puts two fingers on my lips. "I'm sorry I ever agreed to that. I was trying to…protect my heart. It was dumb and it didn't work anyway. I love you. I don't want a thirty-day review. I want to give you everything I am and let you take care of my heart. I think you'll do a better job with it than I did." She takes a deep breath. "I want to go get the test out of the bathroom. Make sure it's real." She points to the bed. "You get naked. And…right back I'll be."

Epilogue

Boone

Five Years later

I'm wearing a hole in the carpet of the honeymoon suite as I pace. I haven't seen my wife in two weeks. We haven't been apart this long before, and it damn near killed me.

I check my watch for the umpteenth fucking time. She's about ten minutes later than we hoped, but there could have been traffic. I know her flight landed on time.

I hear her key card in the lock, and I'm across the room and on her the second she's inside. I push her into the door and my tongue is in her mouth. She whimpers and sags like her legs won't hold her, but I've got her. I won't let her fall. I rip my mouth away. "Never again. I can't be without you that long. It was like being back in prison."

"I'm done with internships now. But if this is the homecoming I get, maybe I should go away more often."

I lean my forehead against hers and groan as my hand slides under her shirt, my mouth finding hers again.

Her back is smooth and soft under my hands, driving me wild. Madeline lifts my shirt, and I hate that I have to break away from her mouth for the time it takes to pull it over my head, but I use one more precious second to remove hers too. I want to stare at her perfect tits, but she's impatient and already back in my arms, crushing against me skin to skin. Nothing has ever made my knees as weak as the feel of her pressed against me.

But I have to have more.

"Sunshine, we're going to have champagne and talk and all that stuff, I promise." I spent an hour in this suite making it as romantic as I could. "But after." I hope that's okay because I can't think. I just want inside her heat so bad. "Before you ask, Pops is fine, the kids miss you, the farm is running well, and I need to fuck you. And happy anniversary."

"I need you too, Boone. It was too long." Madeline's mouth leaves my lips and slides to my neck. I hold her there tightly, probably too tightly, as she works her familiar magic over my throat. She's going to leave a mark. I can't wait to see it tomorrow.

Being without her really did bring back bad memories. I'd pushed all those years of lock-up aside, but without her next to me, every night was an eternity of remembering what it was like without her. Without love. If I didn't have the kids, I would have gone insane, but they kept me grounded.

Right now, I have the world in my arms, and I am going to commit to living like I've never done before.

Her teeth scrape over my pulse point, and I groan, planting my legs wider so I won't fall down. "Jesus, you're going to kill me."

Her hands brush over my back and down my sides with feather-light touches that raise bumps over my flesh. She touches me with random strokes, so I can't anticipate where her touch will land next, only that it will be like small puffs of oxygen on coals that are just ready to ignite.

I wrap her hair around my hand and pull so that she is forced to tilt her head up and away from my neck. Her stormy eyes watch me curiously. The smattering of freckles across the bridge of her nose tugs on the strings of my heart. "You are so fucking beautiful."

She starts a smile that I greedily steal in a deep kiss while I pick her up and carry her to the bed. I lower her to the middle of the bed and yank her pants off. Pulling both her wrists above her head, I pin them against the mattress in one hand. "Stay," I command.

Because, *fuck*.

Madeline responds by arching into me, brushing her damp panties against my cock still trapped in my jeans. I groan and pull away, keeping a firm grasp of her wrists. I want this to last.

I'm eyeing her body, so tempting with all its curves and softness, and wonder where to start.

All the words bunch up in my throat, choking me with emotion. I rest my cheek against her breast and listen to the steady beat of her heart. I press another kiss to her pebbled nipple and grin as a tremor shakes her body. The next kiss on her tit is harder, wetter, and ends with a nip so that she shudders and moans.

"Boone, let go, I want to touch you."

"No," I answer, ignoring her protest as I gather her other breast, first in my hand, and then into my mouth.

"I love your tits, baby."

She arches, and her hips rub against my cock, but I pull myself away. She has the power to turn this long-waited for night into a display of me coming buckets in my own pants. I need to keep control right now, as much as I want her touch.

My grip on her wrists tightens as she writhes under my kisses. Somehow, I manage the buttons of my fly, and I'm sure it isn't pretty, the way I'm kicking off the jeans, socks, and shoes, but it feels a hell of a lot better to be free. My dick is pointing to her like she is the only direction my compass knows.

"Please," she says when she gets an eyeful of me. Male pride rushes through me. She's always been fascinated with my cock, so I run my hand down the length of it while she squirms to be closer.

"What's your rush, sunshine?" I love that she wants me so much.

I move to her side so I can access more of her body without giving her back her hands. Letting go of my dick, I lean lower, tracing the seam of her panties with my tongue. She smells so good. Like honeyed fruit. And home. And love.

I need to taste her, to feel her against my tongue. I rip the scrap of fabric that separates me from my prize. She is so beautiful, glistening with feminine arousal. Dipping my mouth into her, she rewards me as she cries out a sob of relief even as she bucks against my firm hold on her wrists.

"So sweet," I tell her. Better than the finest wine, my girl. I want to tease and taunt this pussy, bring her to a slow-building orgasm, but her fevered pleas ringing in my ears and the incredible flavor of her against my tongue unite against me. The muscles in my arms and shoulders begin to shake in protest—I didn't realize I've been clenching them so hard. Trying to keep her still below me, trying to hold myself back from plunging into her. Every nerve in my body is raw and seeking.

And just like that, I lose control. Instead of pleasing licks and nibbles, I become an animal between her thighs. I growl like a beast and suck at her greedily, not letting up as she comes hard, crying out my name.

"Again." I go back down and use my tongue in her pussy like it's my dick, avoiding her clit for now, remembering how sensitive it is right after she comes.

"I can't."

"I need more of that sweet cream, baby. I need you to come on my tongue."

"Yeah, well, I need you to fuck me."

I nip the inside of her thigh. "You want my dick, you come on my tongue."

I go back to licking her as she bucks against me. She's never been this wet or this vocal. I can't slurp her up fast enough. I'll never get enough.

"Oh, God," she wails and humps against my face until I feel all the tension from her body release.

"That's my girl. Giving me everything. Such a sweet and tasty treat." I move back on top of her and she wraps her legs around me, pulling me to her heat. "Please." Her eyes convey a deeper meaning than words can say. "Please."

I slide into her body, still holding her down with one hand and pausing as she stretches around the head of my cock. I hold still. Very still. Looking into her eyes, seeing my own love and need reflected back at me, feeling her heat cling to me.

"You're so tight. Oh, baby." Nothing has ever felt so good as being inside my wife.

I need to slow us down or I'm going to start thrusting too hard. I pull out and we both gasp.

"You're such a tease, Boone."

"You're just cock-hungry, Madeline. You have been since the first time, haven't you?"

She moans. "Please give it to me. God, I need you so much."

I can only agree. But teasing her is second only to coming inside her tight cunt on my list of favorite things.

"You're so hungry for this cock, baby, then show me." I move up, my knees straddling her upper body and trapping her arms against her. "Have a taste of us. Show me how hungry you are."

She opens her mouth, and I feed her my cock that's dripping wet and fresh out of her pussy.

"You're so hot. Fuck. Look at you, gobbling my cock, licking your own juice off me."

She pulls her mouth down until it's just the tip in her mouth and she works her tongue over the slit on my dick, getting as much of my pre-cum as she can. Greedy girl.

"You're going to make me come."

I groan and pull out of that hot, wet mouth. I love how dirty she is with me. Dirty and sweet.

"Give it back, Boone."

"I'll give it to you, little girl. I promise."

But I move back down between her legs instead of her mouth. I let go of her wrists, hissing with pleasure as her nails score my back. Holding her legs open, I shove into her hard.

"Yes," she cries. "I've missed this so much."

I slam into her again. "You going to take it, baby? As hard as I want to give it to you?"

"Yes. God, yes."

This goddamned world sometimes takes more than it gives. But not Madeline. She always gives me everything, and I am just enough of a bastard to take it all.

We move as one, dancing closer to the edge of the cliff that calls to us. She is slick and tight and mine. I slip a hand beneath her, stilling her hips, holding her against me.

She moans, but I need to keep this moment close, prolong the perfect feeling. Her inner muscles clench around me, and I nip her shoulder. "You want something, baby?"

She smiles—a cat ate the canary kind of smile—and tilts her hips just a touch, grinding me against her G-spot.

Hell with finesse. I let go of control and begin to piston in and out of her, the pleasure building as she comes, my name repeated like a prayer on her lips until I can take no more.

I imagine putting another baby inside her. Goddamn. The thought of Madeline big with my baby again adds another layer of lust to our fucking.

"Gonna...have to...fuck, Madeline. I'm close. I need to..."

She digs her heels into me. "Come inside me, Boone. I want you to fill me up. Please God." And then she is screaming and clenching her inner muscles around my cock. Draining me.

The roar that I let out isn't human. It's primitive and raw.

Madeline

"DID WE DIE? I THINK we just died."

Boone flops over onto his back. "Nobody dies until I take you on your hands and knees tonight. Been thinking about that a lot."

"You need to feed me first. You promised."

He smiles at me and brings us a tray of chocolate-covered strawberries and champagne. I call the twins to tell them goodnight and that I'll see them in the morning. Pops tells me not to worry, he's got everything under control.

After I hang up, I look for more food. "Tell me there's dinner somewhere." The last time I ate was...actually, I'm not sure. Time zones and travel have confused me.

"I ordered pizza. It will be here in a few." He kisses my shoulder. "I'm so proud of you, baby. For finishing school. This internship was the last thing, right? Now you graduate?"

"Yep. I'm so glad to be done. I got some good ideas for marketing the farm, though."

He catches me up on the vegetable crop, the state of the pumpkin patch, and the idea he's been working on for hayrides. "I think we can do them in the winter, too. Like a Christmas thing."

The pizza comes, gets eaten, and we make love again. Slower this time.

It's hard to believe how much my life has changed in five years. People did a lot of talking about us. We were never going to make it. We were going to crash and burn.

But here we are. Stronger than ever.

My life was hard before I met Boone, and it isn't always sunshine and roses now. I mean, a farm, twins, and college all at the same time are challenging. But I have a family now. I know what love feels like. I give our kids all the things I didn't get from my dad. My father-in-law is a wonderful grandpa. My husband is a huge badass with a mushy heart.

I guess, in the end, I'm really glad that I was such a horrible waitress. Mad Maddy and the Homecoming King is a pretty good love story.

TRUE LOVE IS AMAZEBALLS, yeah?

If you enjoyed the Blue Collar Bad Boys series, you'll love the *Love in Brazen Bay* series, starting with Leo and Dixie who fall in love by way of a wrong number text. Want a sneak peek of *Wrong Number Text*?

So wrong it's right...

When grumpy firefighter Leo finally answers the wrong number texts he's been getting for several days, he has no idea pixels on a screen could be so hot—make him want things he's never wanted before.

Dixie has always been quiet, shy, and reserved. Until she "meets" Leo. He's got the once shy librarian shedding her inhibitions and growing her confidence in their texts and calls—and it even starts spilling out into her everyday life. Part of her revels in her secret life—but part of her secretly wishes for more.

They never share more than first names, but each texting encounter gets hotter and hotter—and more intimate than either of them ever imagined. But you can't trust a stranger on the phone. Not really. You can't ache for something you've never had. And you certainly can't fall in love with someone you've never even met, can you?

Author Confession: Welcome to Brazen Bay, a small town I crafted just to explore that feeling of *so wrong, it's right*. Just because something is forbidden or taboo doesn't make it wrong, does it? (You'd have to see the pictures on their phones to answer that.) Gruff Leo and sweet Dixie are perfect strangers and perfectly naughty when they let their guards down with someone for the

first time. What starts as an innocent wrong number turns into something much more daring. Bonus points if you read this wrong number romance on your phone.

Chapter One

Leo

DIXIE: HI, TIM. THIS is Dixie from the accident.

Dixie: Please text insurance info you promised.

Two days later

Dixie: Still need insurance stuff. Please?

[...]

I set my beer down. I ignored her texts two days ago. I thought she would just go away. I don't like texting people I know, much less strangers, but it looks like I need to deal with this.

Leo: Tim sounds like an asshole.

Leo: He also gave you a wrong number.

Dixie: Are you serious right now?

Dixie: I hate men.

I smile at my phone. A first for me. I hate my phone. I only ever scowl at it.

Leo: I'm a man.

Dixie: Sorry! It's not your fault.

Leo: If you find him, text me back. I'll beat him up for you.

[flexed biceps emoji]

If the guys at the station knew I was using emojis right now, I'd never hear the end of it.

Dixie: *[smiley]* **My hero.**

Dixie: I wish there were more guys like you.

Leo: My last gf would disagree.

Dixie: Don't ruin my fantasy!!

Leo: You're fantasizing about me already, huh?

Dixie: Sure, LOL. Help me out. What are you wearing?

[heart-eyes emoji]

Leo: You don't want to know my name first, baby?

Leo: I feel so used.

If only it was this easy to flirt with women face to face, I'd be a real Casanova, like my buddy Drew. He does all the swiping and never sleeps alone. I don't actually know what swiping is.

Dixie: JK. I'm not the kind of girl who sexts with strangers.

Leo: My name is Leo.

Leo: There. Now we aren't strangers.

It's a little weird that I have to rub my palm on my jeans. I'm going to blame the condensation on my beer and not that I have sweaty palms from flirting with a stranger on my phone. Too much time goes by with no reply, and now I'm starting to feel like a dick.

Jenkins sets his empty on the bar next to me and taps my shoulder from behind. "Hey, Cap? You're up."

I flip my phone over. Which probably draws more attention to it. Like I'm hiding something. Which I am. "I'm going to finish my beer and call it a night. I'll forfeit this round."

"You sure?"

"Yeah."

Jenkins goes back to the dartboard, and I think about what the hell I'm doing. I must be pretty hard up if I'd rather flirt via text than beat the guys on my crew at darts. I should probably see about getting myself a real live woman instead of pixels on a screen. But something about Dixie keeps my eyes glued to my phone, wondering if she's going to respond.

Leo: Dixie? You still there?

Dixie: Yeah. I think. Nice to meet you, Leo.

Leo: Do you still want to know what I'm wearing?

Dixie: I don't know. I'm—this isn't how I usually am. I'm kind of shy.

I'm strangely aware of my own breath as it quickens. I look around the bar, but nobody is noticing me. My face feels hot. I'm almost forty fucking years old. My days of flirting online should be in my past. I feel like I'm back in 1999 in the first chat room where a woman asked me: a/s/l.

Here goes nothing.

Leo: Do you want to be the kind of girl who sexts with strangers?

I exhale and take a drink.

Dixie: I don't know that either. Is this normal?

Leo: Flirting with a wrong number text? I think it's hot.

Leo: Tell me something about yourself.

Dixie: I'm 23.

Fuck. She's a baby. I should stop this right now.

Leo: I'm 38. What do you do?

Dixie: I work in a library and I'm a grad student.

Oh, man. I love librarians. And she didn't cut me off when I told her how old I was. That's a good sign, right? I almost lied and said twenty-eight.

She's a librarian. Fuck. My pants are getting tight at the thought.

Leo: Do you wear those pencil skirts and glasses? Because that's seriously sexy.

Dixie: If I didn't, I would tell you I do. Since you think that's hot.

I check the mirror behind the bar. The guys are still playing darts in the reflection. Nobody is paying attention to me.

Leo: I think you might be a bad girl.

Dixie: I think you just have a thing for naughty librarians.

Leo: God, yes. Brainy girls are hot.

Dixie: What about you?

I could tell her. A lot of women think firefighters are hot. But something stops me. Tonight, I don't want to be regular me. I want to be this Leo, the one who flirts on his phone. The one who isn't always waiting for the next thing he's responsible for to need him, to drop everything and attend to it.

Leo: What do you want me to be?

Dixie: Hmm...anything I want?

Leo: Anything.

Dixie: Well, right now, I'm fantasizing that you're a mechanic because my car is toast thanks to Tim.

Damn. She's cute.

Leo: So you're still fantasizing about me then. That's a good sign.

Leo: What are you doing right now? Besides texting me?

Dixie: Trying to figure out how to find that asshole who hit my car and gave me a fake #.

Dixie: You?

Leo: I'm in a bar. Supposed to be playing darts, but I forfeited my game.

Dixie: So you could text me?

Leo: So I could text you.

Dixie: I feel special.

[smiley]

"Seven Nation Army" comes on the radio, and I'm feeling like I'm twenty-three again myself.

Leo: Are you alone?

Leo: Sorry. That sounded like a creepy line from the serial killer in a movie.

Leo: You're probably going to block my number now.

There's a pause, and I tell Nash behind the bar that I don't want another beer and clear my tab with him. I'm walking out the door when my phone vibrates.

Dixie: I'm alone.

I pause. Hell.

Leo: I've never spent this much time with a wrong number before.

Dixie: What would be different if we met at the bar?

Leo: Well, I'd know for sure what you were wearing.

Also by Brill Harper

Blue Collar Bad Boys
Bounced: A Blue Collar Bad Boys Book
Nailed: A Blue Collar Bad Boys Book
Drilled: A Blue Collar Bad Boys Book
Wrecked: A Blue Collar Bad Boys Book
Laid: A Blue Collar Bad Boys Book
Tagged
Plowed
Bucked: A Blue Collar Bad Boys Book
Banged: A Blue Collar Bad Boys Book
Tapped: A Blue Collar Bad Boy Book

It's Complicated
All Together
All at Once

Love in Brazen Bay
Wrong Number Text
The Right Stuff
So Wrong It's Right

Don't Get Me Wrong

Standalone
Dirty Jobs: a Blue Collar Bad Boys Collection
Notch on His Bedpost
Honeymoon With The Prince::A Modern Day Fairy Tale
Good Girl

Watch for more at https://brillharper.com.